Weymouth Bound

Paul Weston

Roving
Press

© 2012 Paul Weston
www.paulweston.co.uk

Published by Roving Press Ltd
4 Southover Cottages, Frampton, Dorset, DT2 9NQ, UK
Tel: +44 (0)1300 321531
www.rovingpress.co.uk

First published by Rare Device 2010
This edition published by Roving Press Ltd 2012

ISBN: 978-1-906651-176

British Library Cataloguing in Publication Data
A catalogue record for this book is available from the British
Library

Map drawn by Tim Musk
Cover picture is a detail from 'The *Dorothy* Entering Salcombe' by
Mark Myers

Set in 11/13 pt Minion by Beamreach (www.beamreachuk.co.uk)
Printed and bound by Beamreach (www.beamreachuk.co.uk)

For Sally

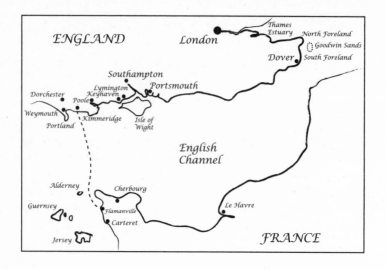

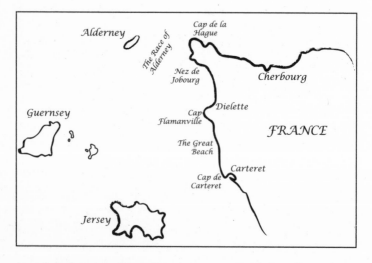

French and English Channel coasts and ports featured in the story.
The dotted line marks Jack's intrepid sail back to England in Jean René.

Chapter 1
Landing

The night was moonlit, and though we were close enough to the shore to hear the waves breaking on the rocks, the drizzle prevented us from seeing anything more than occasional glimpses of the land. I hung over the stern while my father rowed, my hand feeling the tension in the grapnel line dragging astern. We'd been rowing back and forth for three hours, and I was wet through and cold. I felt the line snag. At last!

'Something here.'

Father stopped rowing and lay on his oars, wiping the rain from his eyes. We seemed to be in our own small world, everything dripping moisture. I pulled the rope steadily, bringing the first tub of brandy and its stone weight to the surface. Father lifted it over the side, cut the weight free and lowered the barrel into the bottom of the boat.

The boat was full of kegs when we heard a faint sound, just a soft hiss above the noise of the swell breaking on the rocks. We both looked up and peered through the drizzle.

'There,' father pointed, 'the *Alert*.' I looked and saw the Revenue cutter in the moonlight. She was almost upon us, startlingly close, moving quickly despite the light wind. Despair swept over me. 'She hasn't seen us,' he said, but the edge in his voice betrayed his words, and as he spoke there was a shout from the cutter's deck and she altered course towards us.

Father's face was a study in despair. There was too much contraband to hide, no time to throw it overboard, and it would float anyway now that we'd removed the weights. I saw men move on the cutter's deck, reducing sail.

A voice hailed us, loud and clear. 'Hold water there, and come alongside us.' The cutter's crew had all the sail off her now, except for a scandalised mainsail, and she was almost stopped. She was not towing a boat, but there was one on her deck.

Father spoke urgently through clenched teeth. 'Get down in the boat, Jack, lie down on the boards!' and suddenly dug in his oars, pulling with all his strength towards the shore. I looked up at him. The appearance of the *Alert* had been frightening, but what upset me most that night was the sight of my father as he rowed for his life with his feet braced against the thwart in front of him. There was a wild, frightened look in his eyes, his lips were pulled back from his teeth in a horrible grin and the veins bulged in his neck. He was rowing the boat faster than I had thought possible, heading towards the shore, but it was a large boat and heavily laden. I peeked above the gunwale and saw the cutter making sail again and turning slowly to intercept us. There was another hail 'Stop in the King's name!', but my father did not vary his stroke.

We were about a hundred yards from a large offshore rock perhaps thirty feet high, and I realised that he intended to get close into the shore where the deep-keeled cutter could not go.

There was another shout which I could not make out, and then a series of bangs from the cutter as the men on her discharged their muskets. We were nearly at the big rock when the atmosphere was suffused by a red glow, there was a louder bang, and we heard shot screaming over us through the rain.

'The swivel,' father gasped, and then the rock was abeam and he rowed the boat behind it. Though the wind was light, there was quite a swell round the base of the rock, and I could hear the backwash sucking round other unseen dangers nearby. Father rested on his oars, gasping for breath, allowing the boat to drift backwards and forwards on the surge.

'Water,' he said between breaths, and I felt around the boat until I found the bottle. He took a great swallow and wiped his brow. 'We'll go up the coast well in and strike across the bay when we get to Ringstead. Wind's against us, so I'll row. You go up in the bows and look out for rocks. Cutter can't get in here, it's a thick night, and she doesn't know where we're headed. We'll be all right, Jack, don't worry.' He patted my shoulder and, though his words were reassuring, his voice shook.

As he drank, his face was lit by another flash, followed by the bang of the swivel. Looking over his shoulder he handed me the bottle and with a great heave on the oars got the boat underway. We went along the coast for an hour, creeping through the off-lying dangers. Occasionally, despite our best efforts, the boat bumped on rocks, and once she went aground on the top of a wave and I had to jump overboard into the cold water and push the boat off the slippery surface when the next big wave came.

We saw and heard no more of the cutter, which was just as well for we were all in when we finally got to the high cliffs of Ringstead, set the sail and headed across rainy Weymouth Bay for Portland and home.

***

The Isle of Portland juts out into the English Channel, connected to the Dorset coast by a narrow causeway of shingle. I am a well-travelled man now and understand why outsiders often see Portland as a grim place, windswept, barren and steep. For mariners, Portland is dangerous. The English Channel, as though affronted by the obstacle in its path, boils and churns terrifyingly in the Race at the tip of the Isle. The Race has claimed the lives of countless sailors, and many more have perished yards from the shore in the undertow of the Chesil Beach, a pitiless lee shore.

Portlanders are a breed apart, suspicious of outsiders and with a curious, uneasy relationship with the sea. Women with seafaring husbands, half woken on winter nights by the gale howling round their cottages, reach out for comfort, and finding none there, come fully awake and pray for their husbands' safe return. Others listen to the gale with satisfaction, knowing that the morning will bring a rich harvest of wreckage on the iron-hard beach.

For most Portlanders the choice of occupation is limited to sea or stone. I came from a seafaring family and as soon as I was able to handle an oar and trim a sail I became a fisherman, like my father and his father before him. Our boat, patched and often repaired, was vital to the family. Fishing was not its only employment though, and we were prosperous by local standards.

In those days Portland was almost lawless, and smuggling was carried on to an extent scarcely conceivable today. Often our night-time fishing expeditions took our boat alongside a dark vessel showing only a dim blue light, and I would help father stow packages and kegs in the bilges – a perilous occupation, and more than once I heard the creak of the Revenue cutter's rigging, the rush of her bow wave, the shouted challenge and crack of her Carron, and counted myself lucky to escape the Revenue's shot or the journey in fetters to Dorchester Assize.

Some Portlanders never left the Isle, but I was not one of those. When the wind served we often went to sell our catch in the port of Weymouth. Sometimes my father traded goods more lucrative than fish, and this other business was frequently conducted in the dark and smoky taverns along the quay. Despite being a Portlander, whose morals are supposed to be lax, he would not allow me to accompany him into the taverns, and I spent my time wandering along the busy quay looking at the ships working their cargoes alongside.

The world has changed in my lifetime, and I suppose I have done more than most to change it. In those days there was not a paddle wheel or funnel to be seen in Weymouth Harbour, or indeed anywhere in the world. Ships were driven as they had been since the beginning of time, by the power of the wind and the muscles of men. The ships alongside the quay in Weymouth were a fascination to me, their names, exotic ports of registry and the men who worked them, and I wanted above all to become a sailor. I was worried father would never allow me to go away to sea, and that I would have to run away if I was to fulfil my ambition, something that I could hardly contemplate.

Father, though, had not been a fisherman all his life. He had spent several years before the mast in merchant ships and had been as far abroad as Holland, and France in time of peace. He knew I was fascinated by the ships in the harbour, and I realise now that he was intent on getting me away from the dangers of contrabanding.

One summer evening, when I was fifteen years old, he took me with him to the Ship Inn on the quay at Weymouth. The tavern was crowded with sailors, workers and women of the port, thick with tobacco smoke and noisy with music and singing. I followed him to a table near the back of the room, at which was seated a well-dressed man about forty years old. The man nodded in greeting and indicated that we should take seats on the opposite side of the table.

My father spoke. 'Jack – this is Mr Wellstead, part owner and master of the *Cicely*. Mr Wellstead, my son Jack.' That my father's tone was so easy with a person whose standing would not normally lead him to associate with a fisherman came as no surprise to me. In those lawless days, father's success in the contrabanding trade gave him what almost amounted to respectability. He was a useful man to know.

I'd seen the *Cicely* often enough in the harbour. She was quite large, a topsail schooner of three hundred tons or so, registered in Weymouth, unusual because of her largely fore and aft rig. A proper ship, trim and well kept up. Meeting her master awed me considerably.

I stammered, 'Pleased to meet you, Mr Wellstead.'

Wellstead smiled and inclined his head.

My father spoke again. 'Mr Wellstead here has offered to take you on as his apprentice. I know you'd like to try the seafaring life, as I did, and don't think you should pass up the opportunity he's prepared to give you.' I was amazed. This was wonderful news, wonderful. I couldn't speak, only managing to nod my head vigorously.

Wellstead spoke for the first time. His voice was deep with a pleasant Dorset accent. 'Before you make up your mind, Jack, would you like to look round the ship? We'll go there now if you'd like to.'

Like to? 'Yes please, sir' was all I could say.

Wellstead stood, picked up his old-fashioned three-cornered hat and led me out of the tavern. I glanced behind at father, who was still sitting at the table. He motioned to me to go on and I followed Wellstead as he picked his way out of the crowded room, with not a few 'Good evening, sirs' from the customers.

I walked behind him as he strode along the quay to the ship, basking in his reflected glory. He was clearly a man well known and respected in Weymouth.

We walked along the gangway and onto the *Cicely*. I was used to our small fishing boat and the *Cicely* seemed huge and substantial in comparison.

'We've finished loading,' Wellstead told me, 'a cargo of stone and hay for London. We'll sail tomorrow morning.' As he spoke he glanced up at the sky, in what I later realised was the conditioned reflex of the seaman relying on the weather for his livelihood.

Wellstead showed me round the ship, displaying as he did his pride of ownership, obvious even to me in my excitement. He pointed out masts, great spars with their furled sails, anchors, the wheel, hatches, rigging and belaying pins. He showed me the fo'c'stle where the crew lived, the galley, and took me into the cabin aft where he and the Mate had their quarters.

Wellstead told me to sit down at the table in the cabin,

placing himself opposite me.

He looked straight into my eyes. 'What I want, Jack, is someone who can learn quickly and help me in my business. There's a lot to know, and the life's pretty hard, but she's a good ship and there's great prospects for you if you stick to it. We'll be back in Weymouth in a month or so, and I'd like you to join us then.'

I remember the walk back along the quay in the warm summer evening, my feet scarcely seeming to touch the ground. I was to go to sea, not by running away but with father's consent and encouragement, and not as a common sailor but as an apprentice, a person with prospects. I saw my father standing outside the tavern and smiled at him. He walked forward and embraced me, and we sailed back to Portland, talking excitedly of the *Cicely* and her master.

Early in the morning a month later I was standing with father on the quay at Weymouth, looking at the *Cicely*, recently returned from London. It was May 1800 and my seafaring life had begun.

Chapter 2
The English Channel

Nowadays, with iron steamers, electric telegraphs and railways it is difficult to remember that within living memory the coasting trade of England was largely conducted as it had been in the time of Drake, and for all I know when the *Pax Romana* held sway over these islands.

Probably the average coaster was larger than in Drake's time, and her rig and gear more efficient, but the improvements had been slow and gradual, and England's great admiral would have had no trouble in stepping aboard the *Cicely* in Weymouth that morning, and taking her up Channel as he had done with the ships of his own youth. As it was for the ship, so it was for the men. Though the *Cicely's* crew were nearly all Weymouth men, I think that Drake would have found little difference between them and the Devon crews of his youth hundreds of years before. The lot of the sailorman was hard and dangerous, but the *Cicely's* men were settled and contented, and they had mostly been with the ship and Mr Wellstead for many years. Confident in their trade, handed down from time immemorial, they did not know of the changes that would make them almost the last generation of English seamen to ply their trade in wooden sailing ships.

Mr Wellstead met us on the deck, and we went into the cabin. On the table was a clutter of papers, and Wellstead cleared a space and took out a large scroll from a drawer. I knew what it was, the Articles of my Apprenticeship. My father made his mark, and Wellstead and I signed. My mother had insisted on teaching me the letters which she herself had learned as a child, and I am sure that if she had not Wellstead would not have taken me as his apprentice, despite his friendship with my father. Wellstead was now my master, and I his apprentice, for the next seven years. My fate was sealed. He shook my hand and then, to my great astonishment, so did my father, something he had never done before, and never did since. We all left the cabin and walked along the quay to where our fishing boat was tied up. Father got into the boat and, with the breeze blowing off the quay, hoisted the sail. At my father's nod Wellstead and I pushed the boat off the wall and the lugger gathered way as my father sheeted in the sail. I watched the boat with tear-clouded eyes until he bore up for home at the end of the harbour.

Wellstead clapped me on the back. 'Come on, Jack, we've work to do. We're only going to London, and we'll be back in Weymouth in a month or two.'

He was right, there was work to do. I was given over to the charge of Harry, the bosun, a grizzled old 'shellback' with clear blue eyes in a bronzed, wrinkled face. A golden ring sparkled in his left ear and his hair was pulled back into a tarred pigtail. For the next two weeks while the ship lay alongside the quay at Weymouth I painted, greased and cleaned under his watchful eye. He made me climb high into the rigging, which did not frighten me as much as you might suppose, and constantly bombarded me with the names of the parts that went to make up the sweet harmony that is a well-found ship.

I was a good pupil, anxious to learn, and the knowledge I had gained handling small boats put me in good stead. Harry had not always been a coasting man, and he told me unbelievable stories of the sea and the things he had seen on his voyaging. My thirst for adventure increased with the telling of each tale, and I lay awake in my bunk in the fo'c'stle imagining adventures in far-off lands.

The cargo was blocks of Portland stone, already secured low in the hold, and hay for the horses of London, to be loaded on top of the stone. The hay was brought down to the ship in a procession of heavy farm carts. I felt immeasurably superior to the farm boys driving the carts. Wellstead supervised the loading of the ship, but was frequently away from her. He had a house in the town, where he slept, and sometimes would come down to the ship with his wife, a well-dressed and striking looking woman. Many of the crew likewise had homes locally, and it was only those who had nowhere to go to that lived in the fo'c'stle, generally spending the evenings ashore in one of many taverns along the quay. The ship's galley was cold, and I lived on bread and cheese bought in the town.

Eventually hay filled the hold, enough it seemed to me, who had never been further than Weymouth, to feed all London's horses for years to come. The hatches were closed and covered with sailcloth tensioned by wooden wedges. Harry told me, with the shellback's characteristic glance at the windward sky, that we would be sailing early next morning. I went to my bunk that evening so full of excitement that I could hardly sleep, to be woken what seemed like minutes later by the sound of voices and footsteps on the deck.

When I went out on deck the ship seemed to have come alive. The crew, I later learned there were ten of them, had joined the ship, and Wellstead was standing near the wheel, talking to Harry. As I drew near I heard Wellstead say to Harry, who was walking away, 'We'll just have to go without him.'

Harry came up to me and said, 'Ready to go to sea young 'un? Stick close to me and I'll tell you what to do.' He moved onto the foredeck. Men were gathered round the capstan, and I saw that wooden bars had been put into the holes at the top of the drum. Wellstead, by the wheel, waved to Harry who said simply 'Go on then, lads' to the men at the capstan.

I knew that ships entering Weymouth dropped an anchor in the stream before going alongside the quay, so that they could haul themselves off when they left. Harry gave me a little shove, and I took my place at a capstan bar and pushed with the men. I am not sure that my slight weight made much difference, but slowly the capstan turned, the pawl clicked and the great anchor cable rose dripping from the sea, pulling the *Cicely* out into the channel.

At that moment there was a shout from ashore and everybody on the ship turned to see a thin man running along the quayside.

Harry ordered "Vast heaving' and the men laid off the bars. I heard one them mutter 'Leave the bastard on the quay!', leading to grunts of approval from the other men. They were to be disappointed. I have heard the expression 'pierhead jump' used many times to describe almost missing a departing ship, but in all my time at sea since that morning I have never seen it so accurately describe joining a ship in a hurry. As the men muttered to themselves, the running man jumped across the widening gap, legs still pumping and arms flailing, and thudded onto the deck.

Harry gave the man a withering look and turned to the men at the capstan and said with heavy irony, 'Mate's aboard, come on lads'. The men began to push again against the bars. As the capstan turned I was able to look at the man who had jumped aboard. He was lying like a pathetic bundle of rags on the deck, but not one of the crew went over to his assistance. As the capstan turned again the man slowly got to his feet, walked unsteadily aft along the deck and slammed the cabin door behind him.

After a great deal of hard work at the bars Harry shouted to Wellstead 'Up and down', meaning that the ship was now directly over the anchor. Wellstead answered with 'Main topsail' to the men aloft, and as soon as the great sail came billowing down there was a further series of confusing orders to Harry. 'Lee braces' was the only other command I definitely made out, but they were obviously clear to Harry, as he and the men moved quickly and surely around the ship, pulling on ropes and belaying them as the sail cracked in the wind and began to draw. Wellstead spun the wheel and the ship turned slowly in the stream and gradually gathered way.

Harry and the men moved quickly back to the capstan and we pulled the anchor out of the sea. Wellstead next shouted

'Get the mizzen on her' and the crew moved aft and tailed on peak and throat halyards in turn, gradually lifting the mizzen sail. Soon this sail too was drawing, and the quay began to slip past with growing rapidity. Harry turned to look at Wellstead, raising his hand and declaring 'Nice work' to himself.

We cleared Nothe Fort at the entrance to the harbour as the sun rose. A man climbed down onto the dangling anchor and tied a rope to one of the flukes and we hauled it up level with the deck and secured it. Wellstead left the wheel to one of the men and came forward to speak to Harry. Wellstead was a great believer in the adage that a fair wind was not to be wasted, and we got sail on the ship without delay. Looking back, I don't think that I was much use to my shipmates as we made sail for that first trip up the Channel. Ropes were thrust into my hands and I pulled on them, but I did not always know to what the ropes were connected. The men went quietly about their business, and as more sail was set, the *Cicely* heeled as she picked up speed before the quartering breeze. She ran rapidly across Weymouth Bay, the bright sunlight making rainbows dance in the crashing bow wave. To port I saw Weymouth's curve of yellow sand, with the striped bathing machines already carrying the resort's aristocratic visitors into the surf for their morning water cure. Stretching out ahead was the familiar outline of the Dorsetshire coast, high and rugged, and astern the hulk of Portland.

Though I was his apprentice, Wellstead considered that I should know all of the work to be done in every part of the ship, and my duties were often of a menial nature. My first task after sail was set was to help the cook prepare dinner in his galley near the fo'c'stle. The quality and quantity of food is of great importance to seafaring men, even in these days of regulation by the Board of Trade. In this respect, the *Cicely* did better than most. John, the cook, the oldest man in the ship, was small and wrinkled and seemingly hardly handicapped by the hand he had lost at the Battle of the Saints, in the *Barfleur*. His stories were so interesting that my turn in the galley seemed only too short, and I subsequently looked forward to working there.

The crew was divided into two watches called Port and Starboard. The system on the undermanned *Cicely* was 'watch and watch' – six hours on and six hours off. There were three 'dayworkers' – Harry, the Bosun, John, the cook, and me, the apprentice. I soon came to realise that 'daywork' was a rather poor description of my working pattern, as I was frequently called at any hour of the night when an extra hand was needed, and 'all night in' was a state of affairs imagined rather than experienced.

On that day the Starboard watch had the first spell of duty, and it was replaced at twelve by the Port watch which had just had dinner. As I helped John dole out the food to the Port watch I noticed Wellstead leave the deck and go down into the cabin. Shortly afterwards he re-emerged, followed by the Mate, who looked pale and rumpled. I looked at John, who motioned me into the galley and spoke to me in a low voice.

'That's the Mate, Dennis Vasey, a bad lot. He has the Port watch, when he's sober. Last trip he near had us onto the Atherfield Ledges, and would have done for the ship if Harry hadn't come on deck for a breath of air. He's bad when he's sober, but when he's taken drink he's the very devil.' I didn't ask about the Atherfield Ledges, but I inferred from his tone that they were not welcoming.

'Why does Mr Wellstead put up with it?' I asked. I still had not brought myself to refer to the ship's skipper as the 'Old Man' as everybody else seemed to.

John tapped his nose. 'Business. Wellstead doesn't own all the ship, Vasey's father owns some shares. Won't sell to the Old Man.' He was about to say more but checked himself as the Mate appeared at the galley door, looking in with bloodshot eyes, which narrowed when he saw me.

'Ah, our master's new apprentice. Son of a fisherman I hear, but can read and write. Well, we'll see. Bring my dinner to the cabin, boy, and be quick about it.'

John put food onto a square plate, covering it with a cloth, and I carried it into the cabin. Vasey was sitting at the table and I went to put the tray down in front of him. As I did so the ship rolled unexpectedly and some of the gravy spilt from the plate and onto his trousers. His reaction was beyond anything I could have imagined. He roared with anger and leapt to his feet, knocking over the chair as he did so. He grabbed at me with a look of hatred in his eyes, but I dodged out of the way and he stumbled over the fallen chair. I was utterly terrified and ran for the door, straight into Wellstead who was coming in. Wellstead stood in the doorway and took in the scene, me trembling and Vasey struggling to his feet for the second time that day. 'What happened here?' he demanded.

'Your clumsy fisherboy spilled food all over me,' panted Vasey.

Wellstead gave no direct reply but declared in a formal voice, 'Take over the deck if you please, Mr Vasey. St Catherine's north-east distant two leagues, tops'l breeze from the south-west, all plain sail set.' As Vasey left the cabin, Wellstead motioned for me to leave, which I did without further encouragement, wondering at what I had just seen and heartily frightened by it.

I felt recovered after I had had my own dinner, and when I had eaten Harry sent me to the foretopmast with Nat, one of the younger hands. Lookout was to be one of my frequent duties aboard the *Cicely*, for my young eyes were keen and my time fishing had given me a good knowledge of the different types of ships to be met with in the Channel. A good lookout was kept aboard the *Cicely,* not only against the normal hazards of collision, but also for any French privateers or warships which might evade the Royal Navy's blockade of French ports, and indeed for the Navy itself, as the *Cicely's* sailors had a well-founded fear of the press gang.

As the ship forged steadily eastwards, I watched the high cliffs of Dorset slip astern, to be replaced by the lower land of Hampshire, and then the chalk cliffs of the Isle of Wight. I am sure that all who have sailed this way will agree with me when I say that the southern coast of England is as glorious a sight on a sunny summer day as any coast in the world.

By evening the Wight was low behind us on the horizon and the coast of England was almost invisible to port. When I was shaken from my sound slumber I could see in the morning light that the *Cicely* was off the desolate shingle of Dungeness, and that the fresh south-westerly – 'a tops'l breeze', as Harry called it – was still holding. Soon we were sailing through the cutters off Folkestone offering the services of London pilots to ships whose masters were unsure of the road, and I could make out the French coast low on the horizon to starboard. We passed Dover, the white cliffs gleaming in the morning sunlight, and wore round under the South Foreland. I could see hundreds of ships, naval and merchant, anchored off the shore. As I was looking at the sight, Wellstead came up to me.

'The Downs,' he said, 'favourite place for ships to wait. It's a good anchorage, protected from the west.' He indicated the anchored ships. 'They could be waiting for a bit of east in the breeze to take them down channel, or for orders, and those over there by that frigate,' he pointed at some larger ships near a warship, 'are probably forming a convoy to go to the Indies.'

Wellstead was an enthusiast for learning and for modern scientific innovations. In those days many mariners occupied in the coastal trade navigated only by the knowledge they had accumulated over many years' service, and disdained charts. Wellstead, though, was the possessor of several of the new charts published by the Admiralty which were based on scientific surveys carried out by skilled naval officers.

He took me into the cabin, and showed me the chart. 'We're here and here's the South Foreland. We have to go up there and round the North Foreland. This is the main danger, the Goodwins just off the coast to the east of where we are. They're rock-hard sand, and a lee shore with this wind, so I'm going to keep well into the Kent coast. Better to go aground there than on the Goodwins, there's not many that survive that.'

Wellstead was always very keen for me to learn the coastline. Before the building of the lighthouses that we have now, the ability to recognise the ship's position from a glimpse of the shore during a break in the mist might make the difference between life and death.

Chapter 3
The Thames Estuary

Just after dinner on the second day the *Cicely* rounded the North Foreland. For a landmark of such importance, the starting point of the most important estuary in the world, it appeared very commonplace, less impressive by far than the headlands of my native Dorset coast. Wellstead looked at the headland and then spoke to the man on the wheel, 'Helm down and bear up.' As the *Cicely* came hard on the wind the men hauled on sheets and braces and the ship heeled to her work, occasionally sending spray from the short steep waves across the deck.

Though the Mate had come on deck at the change of watch, Wellstead remained near the wheel as the ship sailed up the Thames Estuary. Wellstead had showed me the chart and I knew that there was land to the north, but I could not see it. He had told me of the difficulties of navigating the estuary, and I could see on the chart the intricate patterns of the shallow sandbanks which are traps for the unwary mariner. On that clear July day, though, the route to London could be easily discerned by following the steady stream of vessels plying to and from the great port. I was fascinated by the variety presented, and it seemed as though all seagoing life was there. Flat barges and wherries with leeboards and strange spritsails, merchantmen with rigs like ours as well as barques, schooners and ketches of all shapes and sizes. Once we passed a great black ship glistening with new paint as though just from her builder's yard, and Harry told me that she was an East Indiaman, outward bound for distant foreign shores.

As the day advanced we progressed up the estuary, and gradually the northern shore came into view. Evening drew in and I saw a great beacon burning ahead. Harry told me this was the lightship at the Nore, where we would moor for the night. As we sailed near the light I saw a large number of merchant ships anchored nearby and in the distance a group of men of war, with three great ships of the line surrounded by smaller vessels.

Sails were gradually taken in and way reduced, the anchor got ready, and the ship ghosted up to Wellstead's chosen spot under mainsail alone, to the accompaniment of the man in the chains swinging the lead line and calling out 'By the deep six' and 'a half five'. At Wellstead's command the helm went down and the ship put in irons, heading directly into the wind. When he judged she had stopped, he shouted 'Let go!' to Harry on the foredeck and the anchor was carefully lowered. As the ship gathered sternway the cable was paid out until Wellstead judged that the scope was sufficient and, with Harry's experienced hand on it feeling for any sign of dragging, the rope was snubbed and made fast, and the mainsail lowered.

With the ship moored the watches were stood down, only one man being necessary for an anchor watch. I assisted John in clearing up the galley after supper and was rewarded for my pains when he pointed out his old ship, the *Barfleur*, anchored with the naval squadron. He told me of the fight with the French off Guadeloupe when he had lost his hand, and how the great 115 gun French flagship *Ville de Paris* had surrendered in the Battle of the Saints. Later I sat in the fo'c'stle listening to the men talk as they drank French brandy, on which I do not think the King had received his rightful portion, and singing sea songs accompanied by Harry on his fiddle, vowing to bring my guitar on my next trip. I knew many of the songs and sang them at home with my father, but I was surprised by the improvised words to some of the tunes. The main butt of the humour was the Mate, who was regarded with no affection or respect.

Early next morning a river pilot came aboard in answer to

our signal, and we weighed anchor and sailed with the tide up the great river. Smart handling of the *Cicely* was needed as we rounded the bends, and I had little time to admire the view as the river became narrower and more crowded and the buildings on the shore closer together. This was before the great docks were built in London, and ships were berthed either out in the stream, discharging into lighters, or alongside the banks of the river, leaving only a narrow channel for moving ships. The *Cicely's* berth was on the north bank in front of the hay merchant's warehouse. Before the days of steam tugs, getting the ship berthed safely demanded a very high level of skill on the part of the skipper, well-coordinated work by the crew, and a measure of luck to avoid damage to the ship or others nearby. Fortunately the *Cicely* was well endowed in all of these departments, and by two in the afternoon we were safely alongside, just below the crowded Pool of London.

There is no better way to arrive in London for the first time than up the river from the sea. The deck of a ship affords a fine view of the very heart of the city, and the view from the rigging is finer still. From my vantage point in the foretop I could see the teeming life that made up the great city. The river was full of ships, and lighters, barges and boats were everywhere. Ahead of the *Cicely*, in the Pool, there were so many ships that it almost seemed possible to walk dry shod from bank to bank. Upstream of the Pool I could see the grey bulk of London Bridge.

Ashore, at one glance, I could see more people than I had ever seen before in my life, and there was a continuous din of noise, with occasional louder sounds of shouts or hammering. The area round where the *Cicely* lay, since levelled to make way for St Katherine's Dock, seemed to be a mixture of warehouses and buildings, whose purpose I could not guess, and horrible mean-looking houses, huddled close together, with dark-coloured muddy tracks between them. Everything looked dirty and sooty, and even on that summer afternoon the air was filled with the reek of sea coal smoke. The smell of the city and the river was indescribable, and I thought of the clean air of Portland. I realised that my earlier estimate of the length of time it would take for the city's horses to eat their way through the *Cicely's* cargo was in error. Horses were everywhere – pulling huge carts piled with goods and coaches filled with passengers, and sometimes carrying single riders.

As I watched this spectacle from my perch in the rigging, I noticed a well-dressed man arrive at the bank and come aboard, where he was met by Wellstead and immediately taken into the cabin. Shortly after that I saw the Mate appear on deck for the first time that day and, furtively looking round, walk ashore, to be rapidly swallowed up in the human throng. Although I knew that all hands were required to stay aboard to work the cargo, I was not unduly surprised by the departure of the *Cicely's* second in command, for already I knew that he was only marginally involved in running the ship.

Both Wellstead and Harry had impressed on me that I should not leave the ship when we were in London, and I was so in awe of the place that I had no inclination to disobey their order. In any event, by the time I had finished my day's work I was so tired that I was ready for my bunk.

***

The men, however, had stronger constitutions and started preparations for their 'run ashore' as soon as work was finished. I was surprised at the attention the sailors paid to their appearance, donning the painstakingly preserved suits of clothes which appeared from their bags and passing a fragment of mirror around so that each man could carefully arrange his pigtail and its ribbon to best effect.

With my experience of contrabanding, I was less surprised by the bottles and packets which appeared from various parts of the fo'c'stle. I surmised that the men's income was supplemented by the sale of 'free trade' goods ashore, as I knew that a good price could be had for them in London. It did not occur to me to condemn their actions, as smuggling seemed to me a normal part of life. I do not know how much of the brandy, tea and tobacco consumed in London at that time had avoided customs duty, but I am sure that it was a good proportion. The ships were many, the rummagers few and the incentive was high.

The men all knew of my background and made no effort to conceal what they were doing, despite my connection with Wellstead. Although I never heard him speak directly of the matter, I am sure that he was well aware of his crew's selfless efforts to make luxury goods available to the poorer people of London. Smuggling was as natural as breathing to West Country sailormen. Efforts to prevent it would have been as futile as Canute's on the beach, and would have brought the Old Man onto a collision course with his crew, whose loyalty and skills he depended upon. The crew, for their part, kept their activities small in scale and goods were not concealed outside the fo'c'stle. In this way, if contraband was discovered by the rummagers, Wellstead could plausibly deny knowledge of his crew's activities, and the matter could probably be resolved there and then by a small payment in cash.

That evening the *Cicely's* crew went ashore as one group, which my subsequent experience has shown to be the sign of a happy ship. I know that seamen always look back with affection on their first ship, and the *Cicely* was one of the happiest ships on which I have served. As I was forbidden to go ashore, I was given the role of lookout. When the men were ready I went to my place in the foretop, not to search the distant horizon for a sail or land as I had done at sea, but to look out for the preventative men or their spies. I could see nothing suspicious and signalled the all clear to the men waiting on the deck below. One by one they briefly went into the fo'c'stle, picked up their packages and joined their shipmates ashore. I watched them as they walked in a group past the front of the warehouse and then into an alley at its side. Though I kept watching, I did not see them any more in the streets near the ship.

The sun was setting and I was alone on the ship. I felt secure in my familiar place in the rigging as I settled down to watch the activity of the city. About half an hour after the crew had left the ship I noticed the familiar figure of the Mate approaching. He stopped at the quay and shouted 'Ahoy, *Cicely*' several times, waiting for an answer after each hail. After my experience in the cabin I was thoroughly frightened of him and this made me keep quiet, praying that he would not glance up. I made myself as inconspicuous as I could, lying flat on the foretops'l yard, trying to look like part of the furled sail to which I clung. I watched as Vasey got onto the ship, walked round the deck and into the fo'c'stle calling loud 'Hellos'. He emerged from the fo'c'stle and went briefly into the cabin, still calling. When he came out he had apparently satisfied himself that there was nobody on the ship, and he stood on the fo'c'stle head and waved.

I saw movement by the warehouse and watched as a man detached himself from its shadow and walked unhurriedly down to the ship. Though by now I was very afraid and pressed myself as close as I could to the friendly sail, I still had a good view of the deck. The elevation of my vantage point made it difficult to judge the visitor's height, but his strides were long and confident and made me assume that he was a big man. He climbed easily over the bulwarks, giving me the impression that he was a seafarer. His next action surprised me, and only later did I understand it for what it was, the automatic reflex of the naval officer boarding a ship. He turned to face aft and removed his hat. Though he replaced it quickly, shaking his head as he did so, it was off for long enough for me to see that the top of his head was bare and his scalp heavily scarred. I should have felt more secure with two people on the *Cicely*, but the sight of the man's scarred head made me more fearful. The stranger spoke briefly to the Mate and they then set off on what I can only call a tour of the *Cicely*. They started in the fo'c'stle, spending some time inside, and then inspected the anchors and capstan. It seemed to me that the Mate had brought the stranger down to the ship as a potential purchaser, one that he wished to keep away from Wellstead.

Rigging and sails would be of interest to a man about to make a nautical investment and I feared that these would be the next items to be inspected by the stranger and I would be discovered. That the Mate was unlikely to become violent to me in the presence of the stranger did not come into my mind, and I was therefore relieved beyond measure when they went down the ladder into the hold. I decided I could not stay where I was, as I was likely to be discovered when the rigging was inspected. I reasoned that I should go and hide in the fo'c'stle, as this area had already been examined and was unlikely to be the subject of further interest. I climbed quickly down the rigging and had just stepped onto the deck on the side of the ship near the shore when I saw the top of the hold ladder move vigorously and the head of the stranger appeared over the hatch coaming. He moved quickly and with purpose, and I realised that, despite the disparity between my weight and that of the ship, my descent of the rigging had caused noticeable vibrations in the hull. My way to the fo'c'stle door was blocked, and without thinking of the consequences I climbed quickly over the ship's bulwark onto the shore and hid behind some empty barrels piled on the wharf. I could not see the ship, but I heard the Mate climb out of the hold and join the stranger on the deck. They were only a few feet away from me and I could hear them clearly. I was in a perfect state of fear, trembling uncontrollably.

I heard the Mate's voice, anxious and whining, 'What's up?'

The stranger replied, 'Didn't you notice? A vibration, as though there was someone aloft.' His voice was deep and sonorous and his accent strange.

The Mate's voice came again, pleading, 'I didn't feel anything, I checked before you came aboard, there's nobody else here.

23

Wellstead's away at his brother's house and the crew's drinking ashore. Come back and look at the rest of the ship.'

The deep voice sounded again, with barely disguised contempt, 'You're so full of opium you wouldn't feel a regiment of marines tramping over the ship. I don't believe your Captain would go ashore without leaving somebody on watch. Who was it?'

The Mate tried to be reassuring. 'He and I take turns. It's my turn tonight, he thinks I'm aboard. There was an old man ashore as well, paid by the merchant, but I gave him a shilling to buy himself some grog and he's long gone.'

The stranger was still not satisfied. 'He left *you* in charge of his ship, with nobody else?' The emphasis on the 'you' left little doubt that this was not something he would have done in Wellstead's position.

The Mate did his best to sound affronted. 'Of course he did. He's got his fisherboy spy now, but the little bastard's obviously betrayed his trust and cleared off ashore.'

'Fisherboy spy, what do you mean?' There was suspicion in the man's voice.

The Mate self-justifying continued, 'Wellstead's taken on an apprentice, son of a fisherman. Just to watch me. He wants to keep me down. But someone from that class can't be trusted and the little weasel's obviously scarpered off ashore as soon as his back was turned.' To ensure that the point was driven home he repeated in a more confident tone 'Fisherboy scum – could have told him he'd betray his trust.' If he thought that this speech would ingratiate himself with the stranger he was mistaken.

'My father was a fisherman,' was the short reply.

There was a long silence before the Mate spoke again. 'Very sorry, I meant no offence, but the boy's from Portland and I know what they're like from there.'

The stranger said thoughtfully, 'You're certain he's not aboard? I was sure the rigging shook just now.'

The Mate attempted to sound confident but there was

uncertainty in his voice. 'Quite sure, I looked everywhere, there's nobody on board. Come and have a look at the cabin and then we're finished.'

They moved away and I heard the cabin door shut. I stayed where I was for a moment, and then crossed the untidy yard in front of the warehouse to a convenient pillar which I hid behind, my heart thumping. Shortly afterwards I saw the two men walk across the yard and disappear up the alleyway at the side of the warehouse. By now I was utterly terrified of the Mate, and though my hiding place was damp and smelly, I stayed there rather than return to the ship for fear that I would be alone on board with him. I must have fallen asleep for the next thing I remember was waking cold and aching as the crew shambled past, happily singing their favourite song of the moment, 'Hard Times of Old England':

Oh the hard times of old England
In old England very hard times.

I joined the band as unobtrusively as I could and got quickly into my bunk, hoping that nobody would notice that I had been ashore.

Chapter 4
London

I slept soundly for the remainder of the night, and when I was awoken the next morning by the cheerful shout of 'Rise and shine', my fear of the previous evening had receded and I decided to forget what I had seen and heard as best I could, convincing myself that all I had witnessed was the Mate attempting to sell his father's shares in the ship.

Because of the drink taken the previous night, the crew did not work as quickly as usual and more than once Harry had to speak sharply to the men, who had a tendency to slope off and nurse their sore heads. After dinner Wellstead called me into the cabin.

'Jack,' he said, 'the Bosun told me you didn't stay aboard the ship last night as you were told. You must understand that the instruction was given for your own safety, for which I am responsible, and this mustn't happen again. Must say I'm surprised, Jack. It's not something I would've expected from you.'

I should have told him there and then of the events of the previous night, but I didn't. I don't know why; perhaps the terror that I had felt made the episode seem unreal, like a half-remembered nightmare. All I could do was mutter, 'I'm sorry, Mr Wellstead, it won't happen again.'

He made a dismissive gesture. 'It'd better not. Look, boy, I realise it's a big temptation to go off ashore when you haven't seen the place before, but London's a dangerous city for a lad like you if you don't know the ropes. You could disappear here and not be seen or heard of again, and there's nothing I or your shipmates could do to help you.'

'I understand, sir.'

He looked at me and his face broke into a smile. 'Don't worry, Jack, you'll see London. Look, the Bosun's got my watch tonight and I've decided to show you a bit of the town. We'll leave at six. Make sure you're looking presentable, and we'll have supper ashore.'

At six I stood at the rail outside the cabin door, dressed in my best clothes and hair brushed. I hope my mother will forgive me for saying that my clothes were not all that grand, for she'd worked hard to make them. Wellstead came out onto the deck, dressed plainly but very fine, looking every inch the prosperous ship owner. He hailed a passing boat rowed by two watermen, and as it drew alongside told them that he wanted to be taken to the Temple and agreed a fare. We climbed down and sat in the stern. For the first time in my life I was a passenger in a boat and I found paying somebody else to row me an uncomfortable experience. The tide was flooding, though, so our watermen did not have too onerous a task as it swept us up the river.

It was a trip to remember. The evening was warm and sunny and the Thames was crowded with boats and ships of all descriptions. We passed the grim Tower soon after leaving the ship, and the river became thick with moored ships, discharging and loading into square bowed lighters. The south bank was clearly less prosperous than the north, where I could see many fine and substantial buildings. Wellstead explained that the north bank of the river was the boundary of the City of London itself, the commercial centre of England, home to the country's great shipping and trading enterprises. He pointed out the Custom House and Billingsgate Fish Market on the river front.

Before long our boat rushed with the tide under the great structure of London Bridge, and when we emerged from the arch I saw the astonishing bulk of St Paul's Cathedral looming over the lesser buildings. This gave me a feeling of pride, for I knew that St Paul's like many other fine buildings in London was built of Portland stone, carried here in ships like the *Cicely*.

Ships with tall masts could go no further up river than London Bridge, and smaller craft made up the river traffic here. I admired the skill of the lightermen who used the flooding tide to bring their heavily laden craft up the river, using only a huge sweep at the stern and the occasional judicial touch of anchor to control their advance. We passed under Blackfriars Bridge, which Wellstead told me had been built recently to reduce congestion, and then the watermen put the boat alongside some stone steps at the foot of a large grassy area with a collection of ancient-looking buildings.

'The Temple,' Wellstead explained, after we had gone ashore, 'where the lawyers work.'

We walked away from the river up a green slope of gardens, and then through the streets and courtyards of the Temple itself. Despite the late hour I could see clerks working at high desks, piles of paper everywhere. We emerged through large black iron gates onto a busy thoroughfare, which Wellstead told me was the Strand. The street was crowded with people of all stations, and the general impression I got was of purposeful movement. There were vendors of every commodity and the street itself was busy with horse-drawn traffic. I saw courtyards off the main road, which seemed dark and unpleasant, crowded with people. Some of the people looked ragged and poor, and occasionally I saw whole family groups sitting listlessly at street corners.

I think there was too much for me to take in and I was glad when Wellstead led me into an inn. The place was not too crowded and we enjoyed a meal at a table by ourselves. I asked about the poor people I had seen and Wellstead explained that the war with France had had a very bad effect on trade. He told me that although the building of London continued apace, and there was great demand for Portland stone, the depression in trade meant that freight rates were low and the shipping trade was not as prosperous as it had been.

After we had finished our dinner we left the inn and walked westwards along the Strand. When we came to the great church of St Martin in the Fields we turned along Whitehall, and I saw the government buildings, including the Admiralty with its weathervane on top. We passed Downing Street, where Mr Pitt had his residence, and Whitehall turned into Parliament Street. I saw Westminster Abbey and the Parliament buildings ahead. With Wellstead striding out confidently we turned into Bridge Street and hailed one of the boats waiting for custom at the steps by Westminster Bridge.

As we were rowed back along the river I thought about what I had seen. No book or painting can convey the size and variety of London. The huge number of people was something completely outside my experience, as was the contrast in the condition between rich and poor. I had seen children with pinched hungry faces covered in dirt, only yards away from great ladies riding in elaborate coaches. There had been beggars and cripples and blind people, and lawyers, merchants and aristocrats, all mixed up together. Great buildings loomed over horrible crowded tenements. In the middle of it all was the river, the reason for London's existence, its main thoroughfare and highway to the rest of the world which it would soon come to dominate.

What I noticed more than anything was the smell of the place. The experienced traveller will tell of the different smells of cities throughout the world and, blindfolded, could use his nose to determine whether he was in, say, San Francisco or Bombay. Perhaps it is because London is more familiar to me than other cities that the range of odours there seems much greater than in other places. Even the rank stench of sea coal smoke is reduced at night as fires burn down, and in many districts it is replaced by the smell of wood smoke, as the bakers fire their ovens for the morning bread. Wood smoke reminds me of the driftwood fires of my youth on Portland. The noisome smell of crowded humanity is often overcome by the more pleasant smell of trades carried out nearby, and in a single walk I have frequently identified the odours of brewing, leather working, sugar refining and woodworking.

We returned to the ship at about ten o'clock, and I thanked Wellstead and went to my bunk.

***

The next few days were uneventful as I worked with the sailors discharging the cargo of hay. I was not left alone again on the ship at night, and the Mate was seldom to be seen. One day Wellstead took me with him when he went to the shipping agent's office in Leadenhall Street. We walked through Wapping, the slum near the ship, past the Tower and into the City, fast becoming the commercial capital of the world. I saw how the light-coloured Portland stone of the buildings had become blackened with smoke, giving the area a dark aspect. At midday throngs of clerks emerged into the streets, buying food from vendors and patronising the famous Leadenhall market.

Wellstead seemed tense and on edge during our walk, and I wondered what his business was as I waited on an upright leather chair in an anteroom. He appeared about an hour later with a satisfied look, shaking hands with the agent. As we left the building he told me that he had secured an outward cargo at a good rate for Gothenburg.

'It's a long trip, Jack, longest we've done for a year or so, but we've been there several times and I've got a good agent there. I'm hopeful we won't come back in ballast.'

When we returned to the ship he pointed out Gothenburg on the chart. It seemed a very long way away, but I couldn't wait to get going. The news was not greeted with universal joy by the crew, especially ones with families in Dorset. They had been hoping that the *Cicely* would return there immediately from London.

'More days, more dollars,' muttered one of them.

After the hay was discharged, we moved the ship upriver on the tide to a berth at a wharf just below London Bridge. We were assisted in this task by a pilot and lightermen, who made the job seem easy, keeping the crew amused with the caustic remarks they addressed to other river users, despite the heavy rain. Guided by scraps of sail set and backed for short periods, the ship was moved out into the stream, sailed slowly upriver, and then turned on her anchor and 'drudged' stern-first on the tide. This was my first experience of drudging, a common technique on the Thames and other tidal rivers. The *Cicely*'s anchor was kept on a short cable so that it dragged slowly over the river bottom but still exerted enough pull to keep the ship's head up and check her way. As she came near the berth, she was brought up on the anchor, and thin messenger cables were sent ashore by rowing boat. Longshoremen pulled in and made fast the heavy mooring cables which we attached to the messenger ropes, and we tramped round the capstan and warped the ship safe alongside.

The wharf where we berthed was specially equipped for handling stone, with a powerful crane which could lift the blocks out of the hold and straight onto unusual carts pulled by eight horses. When a great building was under construction, demand for building stone was intense and so the wharf worked night and day to discharge the ships and barges. As soon as we were alongside longshoremen descended into the hold, and the work of slinging the great stone blocks and lifting them out of the ship began. Nowadays, of course, the crane would be driven by steam, but in 1800 men's muscles were the motive force.

Despite the lack of mechanical assistance, the work of discharging the cargo proceeded quickly. Wellstead spent long periods at the hatch coaming watching the operation. Harry told me that he was worried that a rope breaking, or carelessly applied slings, could send a stone block crashing straight through the bottom of the ship.

Once the stone was ashore, we sailed the *Cicely* to a berth at Shadwell further down the river, where a cargo of broadcloth was to be taken aboard. The ship had to be handled with great care during this operation, for without cargo or ballast she was very light, making her tender and difficult to steer. Stowing the cargo, which was in bales, was done by stevedores, while the crew worked on the ship and her gear. I painted the ship's boat and learned splicing from one of the seamen.

One day, when the ship was almost fully loaded, Wellstead asked me to accompany him ashore again. As we walked along Fenchurch Street he met a man with whom he was clearly on friendly terms. They talked in a doorway, while I stood apart, letting my eyes wander over the street activity. I glanced down Mark Lane and to my surprise saw the *Cicely*'s Mate talking in an animated fashion to another man. With a start I realised it was the stranger with the scarred scalp who had been on the ship that night at Wapping. I was about to walk out of sight when a barrel fell noisily off a cart behind me. Both men looked up and the Mate recognised me. He spoke to his companion, who moved his head and looked directly at me. I turned and walked away round the corner to where Wellstead was just finishing his conversation, and we walked on to the agent's office.

When we got back to the ship the Mate was aboard. This was surprising as he had hardly been seen during our visit to London, and his duties had been shared between Wellstead and Harry. As I came up the gangway he looked at me with narrowed eyes, making me feel very apprehensive.

I did not disclose what I had seen to Wellstead. I should have done, it would have been easy enough, but I didn't. Later that day he called me to the cabin.

'Jack, you've been in the ship for several weeks now, and I think you've the makings of a seaman.'

'Thank you, sir,' I said.

He continued, 'If you want to progress you'll have to attend to your learning. You can read and write well and you're handy on deck, but there's more to it than that.' He picked up a large book from the table and held it out to me. 'Take this book. From now on you're to write up a journal, without fail, every day. It's to include the ship's position, the distance run that day and wind and weather conditions.' I took the book. 'At ten each day you're to come to the cabin and attend to this duty, starting with the trip to Gothenburg. Navigation's a science, Jack. You must learn it. The world's not standing still and we must apply the newest techniques to our trade.'

I cannot say that the prospect of spending long periods in the cabin writing up a journal greatly appealed to me, but I knew that what he said was true.

At last the ship was ready for sea, the hold crammed with cloth, and the ship and her gear in good order. With the wind blowing onto the wharf we had to haul her off with the anchor as we had done at Weymouth, and it took some smart handling to get her moving down the river. We had been in London for two weeks, and I believe that all the crew were glad to be leaving.

Chapter 5
The North Sea

With the light southerly breeze, the trip downriver was uneventful, and before dusk the Nore was abeam. Wellstead called me into the cabin and I watched as he laid off the course on the chart, using a handsome set of patent parallel rulers. He used dividers to measure the distance and showed me how to write up the results in my journal. We went on deck and he gave the course to the helmsman, and the ship's company settled into its routine of watch and watch, tricks at the helm or on lookout, meals and laughter in the fo'c'stle.

On the fifth morning I was at the helm with Harry watching over me. The breeze had freshened and it was cold, with a lurid red sunrise in the east. Wellstead came on deck, glanced at the sky and walked over to Harry, who nodded and jerked his thumb towards the sunrise.

'Don't like the look of that much,' Harry remarked. 'Wind's freshened too.'

Wellstead nodded in agreement. 'I know, doesn't look nice. We're in for a blow. Make sure she's all tight and secure, give her a pump, rig the lifelines, and get ready to get some sail off her. Plenty of sea room at the moment, let's make sure we keep it that way. We'll head north.'

From my own experience as a fisherman I knew that the broad pattern of weather was often quite predictable. Strong winds frequently came from the south-west, accompanied by rain and grey skies. Following this the skies became blue with broken cloud and the wind went round to north-west. This was not to say that there were not easterly gales and other exceptions to these rules, but this was the usual pattern of weather. The *Cicely* would be in a bad position if she approached the Danish coast just as it was getting dark and the wind became north-westerly, making the coast a lee shore. Though she had a high proportion of fore and aft sails and was therefore more weatherly than a purely square rigged ship, she could not be relied upon to make progress to windward, especially if the sea ran high.

As the day went on, the wind rose steadily and the ship began to heel and move faster. For the first time I heard the roar of a strong wind in the rigging of a sailing ship. Occasional waves came aboard over the bulwarks. All hands were called and sail was taken off her except for the foresails and a heavily reefed mizzen. The ship slowed and her motion became easier. The Starboard watch was sent below, I with them. The fo'c'stle had changed greatly from the place it had been alongside in London. Wet clothes hung everywhere and the decking ran with water. The motion of the ship made moving around difficult, and it was noisy with the wind's moan, the crash of waves and the creaking of the *Cicely's* structure. Despite this tumult, I got into my bunk and slept soundly until I was called with the Starboard watch at six o'clock.

The sight that greeted our eyes as we went out onto the wet deck was desolate in the extreme. The wind had increased and it was now blowing a full gale from the south-west. The waves were very large, topped by roaring white crests which occasionally struck the ship and swept across the deck. I watched as Nat walked aft along the deck, hanging onto a lifeline. A wave with a breaking crest struck the ship, and as the deck was swept to a depth of several feet, Nat grabbed the lifeline with both hands and with acrobatic ease lifted his body clear of the deck until the wave had subsided through the scuppers.

Wellstead was very insistent that the log should be streamed every hour, so that he could determine how far the ship had run, and my first task was to assist the Mate in this task. As I counted the knots the Mate observed the sand glass, saying 'Now' when I was to start and stop counting. As we worked, I was surprised and pleased by his friendly demeanour towards me. Even with reduced canvas the ship was running at nine knots. Wellstead beckoned me into the cabin, and I watched as he plotted the latest estimated position onto the chart.

'Your first gale at sea, first of many,' he said. 'How are you liking it?'

He pointed to the chart and measured the distance to the Danish coast with the dividers. 'Forty miles,' he declared. 'What do you think?'

'Seems a good long way to me, sir.'

'It isn't, Jack.' Wellstead took his eyes off the chart and looked at me. 'It looks very precise on the chart, but be warned, it's all based on us accurately recording our course and speed. If we can't see the land we can't verify our position, and our position is only as good as our reckoning. You must always record what the ship has done. You can rework the figures, but you're in trouble if you've lost the figures to work from.'

He continued, and for the first time I had an inkling of the heavy responsibility of the shipmaster, 'Fast passages are the way to make the ship work and earn our money, but it's all for nothing if we lose her. The wind'll back north-westerly soon, and when it does it may blow hard. The Danish coast is almost featureless, and there are sandbanks offshore.' He pointed at the chart. 'There's no room for mistakes. Landsmen think it's the sea that sinks ships, but they're wrong, it's nearly always the land. Sea room is the mariner's greatest asset. We've sea room now and I don't intend to lose any of it. We'll heave to, take soundings and if they confirm our position we'll stay hove to until there's no danger of approaching the coast with a north-westerly gale behind us.'

He went out on deck and the ship was worn round and hove to, pointing as close to the wind as she would go, slowly forereaching, with the helm lashed. Soundings were taken with tallow smeared on the bottom of the lead weight and the results compared with the depth and sea bottom type which the chart said we should expect at our estimated position. We got 35 fathoms depth of water, and sand and broken shell in the tallow, which agreed with the chart, so we stayed hove to.

Just after sunset the wind backed into the north-west and the sky became clear. The ship was kept hove to, and when I came on deck at six in the morning the wind had moderated. We took soundings, got sail on her and put the ship put back on her course. I was sent to the foretop, and about eight o'clock I saw a feint smudge on the horizon. I excitedly shouted 'Land ahead' down to the deck and was shortly joined aloft by Wellstead, the first time I had seen him in the rigging. He inspected the land with the small telescope he brought with him and gave a satisfied grunt.

'There she is, Jack, bang on the nose.'

By dinner time we were quite close to the land, running along with it on the starboard side. As dusk fell we saw a light, and Wellstead told me that it was the Skaw, the most northerly point of Denmark, the entrance to the Baltic Sea. All night we sailed along slowly under short canvas, and in the morning put the helm up and ran for Gothenburg, arriving off the port at midday when we were approached by a cruising pilot cutter. After some discussion the pilot came aboard from a rowing boat, and with him standing by the wheel with Wellstead we threaded our way through the rock-strewn channel to the town of Gothenburg.

***

By evening we were tied up at a busy dock in the harbour, my first foreign port. Wellstead considered the town a less dangerous place than London and I was allowed to go ashore by myself in daylight, on the promise that I did not go too far from the ship. Gothenburg was an interesting place and I spent most of my time ashore. It was not on the same scale as London, but was busy and prosperous, cleaner and with less poverty. The buildings were bright and many of them had flower boxes in the windows. Canals were everywhere and seemed to be the main means of moving goods around the city. Wellstead told me that the Dutch had built the city, and there was still considerable Dutch influence.

A ship does not pay her way unless she is carrying cargo, and Wellstead made great efforts to secure one, making frequent visits to the agent, Mr van Wyck, in his offices. Gothenburg has never been one of the British seaman's favourite ports of call, but the *Cicely's* crew were frequently ashore, sometimes returning to the ship in a less than sober condition. In those days, due to the excise duty, the price of tea was very high in England, and many of the crew made investments in the local variety, packets of which were distributed in the nooks and crannies of the fo'c'stle. Eventually Wellstead decided to buy barrels of herring, in the hope that he could take the ship to Newcastle, sell the fish and secure a cargo of sea coal for the south coast of England.

The Mate was seldom seen aboard and rumours began to circulate among the crew that he spent his time in an opium den ashore. One of the crew swore that he had seen the Mate go in through the door of a notorious establishment in the town run by an elderly Chinese man.

John, with his wide experience of the world, was firmly of the opinion that the Mate was an 'opium fiend', as he put it, and that his habit accounted for his behaviour. 'I've seen it before,' he said, 'exactly the same as this; happy when they've got it, but raging savages when they haven't.' He continued gloomily, 'He'll be the death of us all, like as not. Once it gets into their blood it's all they can think about. They doesn't care if there's rocks ahead or the ship's on her ear in a gale, opium's the only thing they care about and they'll do anything to get it.'

When the cloth was discharged and the barrels of herring loaded, we put to sea. Wellstead had engaged a competent pilot, and the *Cicely* safely picked her way through the maze of rocks and islets and lifted to the surge of the waves. There was a brisk southerly breeze blowing as we dropped the pilot, set all plain sail and tramped in fine style past the Skaw and out into the North Sea. About four in the afternoon the ship was close hauled on the port tack when the Mate, who had the watch, gave me the task of cleaning out one of the ship's boats which was still slung out on its davits on the starboard quarter.

There were few people about on deck. The crew was tired after the exertions of working the ship through the channel and those on watch, except for the man at the wheel, were sitting out of the wind behind the fo'c'stle house. The dayworkers had gone below for a spell and Wellstead was in the cabin. With rather uncharacteristic kindness, the Mate took a trick at the helm, sending the helmsman forward to sit with his watchmates. I removed the bung, and started to wash the boat out, using a bucket on a rope to get water out of the sea. This is always a tricky task from a fast-moving ship and is not without danger for the unwary. The bucket must be thrown ahead so that it hits the sea on its side and sinks immediately, and hauled up quickly before the rope goes taut and the ship starts to drag it through the water. The wise seaman always makes the end of the bucket lanyard fast to the ship before commencing the operation.

My task was almost completed, but I decided that one more bucket of water was needed to do the job properly. I was standing up in the boat persuading the bucket to sink, when a gust of wind hit the ship. As the ship heeled there was a crack from forward and the topmast staysail began to flog violently. I am still not sure of the sequence of events, but it seemed that simultaneously the stern of the boat I was in dropped, the lanyard of the bucket violently snatched at my hand and I went flying through the air, to land head first in the shockingly cold and rough sea. I was a good swimmer and surfaced immediately, but my mouth must have been open in a scream when I hit the sea for I was choking and gasping for breath. Everything was a confusing mixture of colour, noise and sensation. The black stern of the ship loomed huge, a few

39

yards away, as she rushed on her course, with the blue and red boat from which I had fallen dangling untidily from the davits. I saw the seaweed on the ship's rudder as it lifted from the water and made out CICELY WEYMOUTH picked out in white letters on her stern. I am sure that those who have survived the horrible experience of falling overboard will agree that there is no more desolate sight to a sailor than that of his ship sailing away from him while he swims in the sea.

Swimming amongst them, the waves seemed huge, and stinging spray was constantly dashed into my eyes. I was in an advanced state of shock and fear, sure that my end had come and I would never again see my family and home. I began to recite the Lord's Prayer. But the *Cicely* did not forsake me, and my heart lifted as I saw heads appear over the bulwarks and water boiling round her stern as the helm was put violently up. I have never before or since seen a large ship deliberately gybed all standing, and I hope never to do so again, especially from the vantage point of a swimmer, but it was an impressive sight, and noisy as well. That the masts stayed in her was a tribute to her soundness and the way that she was kept up. So fast was the turn that she still had way on her when she came up into the wind with her canvas either flogging or aback. The crew worked quickly and I watched as the sails were trimmed and began to draw, the ship forging slowly ahead.

I did not know if they could see me and so with considerable difficulty I took off my coat and tried to wave it above my head. This was not entirely successful, as the weight of it made my head sink below the surface, but I persevered as I knew that the head of a man is very difficult to spot even a short distance away if the sea is rough. As a wave lifted me I saw the boat lowered and five men get in her. I was disappointed when the next wave lifted me and I saw that they were getting out again, but this action was explained when I noticed the boat's bung floating near me, not far from the bucket. Soon the men got back in the boat and it pulled away from the ship. I was overjoyed when I saw them heading towards me, as I realised then that they had seen me from the ship and my salvation was assured.

The boat approached me rapidly, its motion violent in the rough sea, and I could see Harry steering in the stern and Nat in the bow pointing towards me. Soon strong arms hauled me like a fish over the gunwale, and I was sitting shivering in the sternsheets with Harry. The boat turned and headed towards the ship, stopping briefly to pick up the bucket and bung.

'We had to come back to get these,' said Harry, indicating the recovered items. 'The Old Man can't spare his shirt for that long,' pointing as he spoke to the white shirt replacing the boat's bung.

'Cookie needs his pans back an' all,' said Nat from the bow, and I noticed that a cooking pot had been brought along in the place of the bailing bucket.

We were soon back on the ship, and I was given a large tot of brandy, the first I had ever tasted, dried out and sent to my bunk. I heard and felt the ship getting back on course, but shortly fell into a deep sleep. When I awoke the day had long broken and it was sunny with a light breeze. I emerged onto the deck and went into the galley where John was working. I was very concerned because I thought that the incident of the day before would count against me – that I would be in trouble for having fallen overboard and caused so much delay and, remembering the flogging mainsail, probably damage as well.

John greeted me in a friendly way. 'Hello, young 'un, how're you feeling?' I told him that I was much better but would like some food if any was going. As I ate bread and cheese he told me what had happened.

'Bloody fool of a Mate, damn him, making you work on the boat by yourself slung out on the davits, all swinging loose in that sea, and letting you use the bucket in that lubberly way.' His eyes were angry. 'I've never seen anything so stupid in all my life, and that's a fact. Bloody opium fiend, scum of the earth they are. If it wasn't for Nat who saw you just after you went over the wall and never took his eyes off you till you was in the boat, and for the Old Man who handled the ship like I've never seen her handled before, you'd have been a goner.'

He went on, more reflective now. 'You're damned lucky, you are, to have such a skipper and ship. Put the helm hard up straight away and gybed her all standing, he did, and didn't do no damage, 'cept that broken mainsheet block. Bloody lucky he didn't have the sticks right out of her, but she's a good ship. I'd like to know how that davit fall came away. Harry says he made it fast himself, when we left Gothy. Proper mystery that is.' He looked at me keenly. 'Did you fool around with it?'

'No,' I said, 'I didn't touch it.'

He continued his account. 'Old Man took the Mate into the cabin when we were underway again. I don't know what he said, but I'm sure it wasn't complimentary, Mate came out looking very shaky. Should have hanged him from the mainyard there and then in my opinion.'

At ten o'clock I went into the cabin to write up my journal. Wellstead questioned me thoroughly about what had happened, asking questions about what the Mate had told me to do, if anybody had been stationed nearby to keep an eye on me, and whether the Mate had told me to tie myself on. He was also interested in how the after fall had come to be slack. I answered as best I could, and after some time Wellstead said, 'Jack, it's your duty to do as an officer tells you, but you must look out for yourself as well. The ship is a dangerous place for a boy. If it wasn't for Nat's sharp eyes and keeping you in sight until you were picked up, you'd have been lost.'

After I had written the weather data and the ship's position in my journal, Wellstead made me write out an account of what had happened. He kept me at the table nearly all that day, writing an essay on the lessons I had learned the day before.

Five days after leaving Gothenburg we arrived off the mouth of the Tyne, and Wellstead decided to take the ship into the river straight away, despite the strong easterly wind which made the entrance dangerous. In an onshore breeze, the sea breaks heavily at the entrance to the river when the tide is ebbing, and so Wellstead decided to wait until the tide was flooding. While we waited he made an intense study of the chart and fixed the ship's position accurately using bearings from conspicuous objects ashore. He would be on his own for the passage into the river, as the weather was too bad for the Tyne pilots to come out to the ship.

At the appointed hour we ran in under plain sail without incident, anchoring at Shields near the mouth of the river.

Chapter 6
Newcastle and Home

The next morning we lowered the boat and four of us rowed Wellstead up the river to visit an agent he knew in Newcastle. I took bow oar and managed to keep up with the men, though I did not contribute much to the propulsion of the boat. There were many ships berthed in the river, mostly colliers loading coal from 'keels' which lay alongside them. The keels, large flat boats, loaded cargoes onto their decks further up the river, and drifted up and down with the tide. I accompanied Wellstead to the agent's offices, and then to the fish merchant he recommended. Wellstead looked very relieved when the merchant agreed to buy the herrings at a good price, as they had represented a substantial investment. After the deal was complete, we went back to the agent and Wellstead negotiated a cargo of sea coal for Poole and Weymouth. He was in good spirits as we rowed him back to the ship, and I was pleased to hear that we would be going home.

The ship's cargo was discharged into lighters and the loading of coal commenced. Now that steamers are common, the dirt associated with this operation can be easily imagined. The coal dust got everywhere, even into the foc'stle and galley. It did not improve our tempers, but the keel men who worked with the coal seemed unaffected, joking and laughing in their almost incomprehensible accents, even though the work of shovelling the coal from the decks of the keels up onto the *Cicely*'s deck was extremely hard.

Newcastle seemed squalid and poor after Gothenburg, but much livelier. The coal trade dominated everything and the abundance of coal had also led to the establishment of large factories on the banks of the river. Soap- and glassmaking were carried out on a large scale. The people who worked in these places and in the coal trade lived in crowded houses which seemed to me as bad as the worst parts of London. As before, there was a ready market for the free trade goods the men had brought from Sweden, mostly tea. Some of the men bought soap to take south with them, as it was much cheaper here than at home. Wellstead was clearly of the same mind. He had been encouraged by the success of his herring venture, and he bought a large quantity of soap which was carefully wrapped and placed on the coal in the hold.

The Mate did not emerge much from his cabin during our stay in Newcastle and I believe he drank heavily. I was not sorry that I saw him very little and I never discussed the man-overboard incident with him.

At last our business in Newcastle was finished and we battened down the hatches, made the ship ready and sailed down the river to the sea. The North Sea passage was uneventful. We waited three days in the Downs for a southwest gale to subside and then, with a brisk north-westerly and every scrap of canvas set, we rounded up under the South Foreland, and headed for home.

It seemed an anticlimax when the *Cicely*'s head was pointed for Poole instead of Weymouth after we had passed St Catherine's Point at the southern tip of the Isle of Wight. As night was approaching, we anchored in Studland Bay, just outside the harbour. As soon as it was light, with the tide flooding under us, we made our way in and came alongside the quay at ten o'clock, near the custom house. We spent a week in Poole discharging some of the coal, and Wellstead and the men made a profit from the sale of the soap from Newcastle. It seemed strange but pleasant to hear Dorset accents again. The Mate went ashore as soon as he could and was rarely seen on the ship until we sailed. Many of the ships alongside us were engaged in the Newfoundland trade, and Wellstead spent considerable time speaking to their skippers and owners, and it was generally believed among the crew that he had a mind to try that trade, which was said to be very profitable.

We sailed from Poole and entered Weymouth Bay at four in the afternoon. I was very happy to see the familiar coast unfold before us and the shape of Portland come into view. The crew felt the same and every task that day was made lighter by the boisterous singing of shanties, accompanied by Harry on his fiddle. The most popular tune was 'Leave Her Johnny', with the crew improvising disparaging verses about the *Cicely* and her officers. The Mate was the subject of most of the ribaldry and his face was set in a tight mask as he pretended not to listen.

> *The Mate can't reef and the Mate can't steer,*
> *Leave her, Johnny, leave her.*
> *But he likes his gin and he likes his beer*
> *And it's time for us to leave her.*

As we crossed the bay I saw a familiar sail heading towards us and I realised that my father had seen the *Cicely* arriving and was intending to meet us. He bore up under our stern, and there was happiness and relief on his face when he looked up and saw me waving at him. We had a brief shouted conversation and arranged for him to come to Weymouth next day to take me home, Wellstead having agreed that I could spend time ashore while the *Cicely* was in harbour.

I noted that the two warships were still at anchor in the bay, meaning that the King was in residence in the town. Despite my travels abroad I still considered that the situation of the town, nestling at the end of the curve of the beach, with the glorious view of the coastline, was the finest I had seen. I have still not changed that opinion, even after fifty years of travelling the world. In all that time, though I had many adventures and amassed great wealth, I have never again matched the elation I felt that day as the *Cicely* ran easily into the harbour at the end of my first trip to sea.

When the ship was safe alongside, the crew was paid off by Wellstead and the men disappeared ashore carrying their bags. I was left alone on the ship and in the evening went ashore and wandered along the quays. I had changed considerably in my months on the *Cicely*; not only was I bigger and stronger, but also the experience of being with a group of men had made me much more mature.

When my father came to pick me up in the boat next morning I could see the pride in his face as I showed him round the ship, and our happiness continued as we sailed back to Portland and saw my mother waiting on the beach for us to arrive.

***

I stayed at home with my parents for several days, describing the things that had happened to me on the *Cicely* in detail. I did not tell them of my swim in the North Sea, as I knew this would upset my mother and I thought that she might prevent me from rejoining the ship. I went fishing several times with father and, although our catches were good, we did not recover any contraband. Father told me that the war with France had had a bad effect on the trade and that the preventative men were very active, with a new cutter, the *Surprise*, frequently patrolling the coast from her base in Weymouth. There had been several incidents when the Revenue had come close to catching contrabanders, and their muskets had wounded two Portland men scrambling up the cliffs near Ringstead.

About a week later I went back aboard the *Cicely* at Weymouth. The coal was almost discharged. Wellstead told me that he had secured another cargo of stone and hay for London, and he had also decided to buy some barrels of good West Country cider to see if he could sell them on his own account. Some of the crew rejoined the ship and we spent several days cleaning the coal dust out of the hold. Wellstead was always insistent that the hold was cleaned thoroughly between cargoes, though this was not popular with the men. He considered that slovenliness led to the build-up of layers of dirt, and a ship with a clean hold was more likely to attract good freights than one with a dirty rat-infested cargo area.

We moved the ship round to Castletown, and the great stone blocks were loaded. The weather was kind and the loading was completed without incident. We then took the ship back to Weymouth for the hay to be loaded on top.

In the light summer mornings before work started I took to strolling from the port through the town. With the King in residence, Weymouth was crowded with courtiers and servants and what I can only describe as the hangers-on associated with the court. Even at that early hour, the bathers were taking the waters and I joked that I should count myself lucky for my accident overboard, making free use of the *Cicely* as a bathing machine, though I firmly believed that frequent use of the privilege was unlikely to be beneficial to my health.

The King was an early riser, and several times I saw a knot of people walking along the sea front. At the centre was a plainly dressed figure who sometimes waved his stick about, and I knew that this was 'Farmer George'. The antics of the people around him amused me greatly. They jostled for position and occasionally scuffles broke out. Those at the front of the knot walked backwards in a most comical manner, and all of them kept their eyes fastened on the King. As might be expected, the influence of the royal presence in town was all pervading. The whole economy of the place had changed and a large part of it was given over to serving the needs of the court. Weymouth had transformed from a simple port into a resort offering the services that fashionable people expected. The shops in the town, which now included a toy shop and a music shop, had changed their hours of business to cater for the King's preference for early rising and they were all open by six in the morning.

I had conceived a great liking for chocolate during my voyages on the *Cicely* and one morning went to one of the new shops to buy some. As I entered I brushed against a man leaving. I muttered an apology, but the man did not stop. Looking round as he left the shop, I realised with a start that it was the man with the scarred head. I was surprised to see him in Weymouth and thought it likely that he had come to the town to do some business connected with the *Cicely*. I watched as he walked down the street and was relieved that he did not look back and see me.

Wellstead spent most of his time ashore, at his house in the town. I was sent several times on errands there by Harry. The house was new and well appointed, but it appeared to my eyes to be overly tidy and had a cold atmosphere. Wellstead had no children, and his wife was seldom seen when I visited. He worked in a large study, surrounded by account books and charts. On one of my visits I sat in the study as he told me how he had gone to sea as a boy, then over many years and by great diligence had worked his way up in the Newfoundland trade, buying first a part share and then a full share in a schooner. He had spent considerable time in America and was a great admirer of the Americans.

'That's the place for a man to get ahead, Jack. It's huge and there are opportunities for anybody if they work hard. Boston's a rich place, and it's already bigger than most places in Europe.' His words made me realise how little I knew of the world in comparison with a man like Wellstead, and the boundless opportunities that were now open to me.

Chapter 7
Keyhaven

We did not see the Mate until the ship was ready to sail. His embarkation was less dramatic than the previous one, and he greeted me in a friendly way as he came aboard early on the morning of our departure. The *Cicely* got under way with a fresh south-westerly breeze. The wind increased quickly and soon became a full gale. As the wind came up, the crew worked to get sail off her. We had passed St Alban's Head two hours previously, running about nine knots, and had almost finished reducing sail and were tidying up. I was working with Harry to coil up the tails of ropes when there was a cry and Nat fell from the shrouds and landed heavily on the deck. He lay there unmoving with his leg at a strange angle and I could see blood coming from a wound on his head. Harry quickly moved to his side and was shortly joined by Wellstead. They knelt and spoke repeatedly to Nat, but he did not stir. Work stopped and all hands gathered round, except for the Mate and the helmsman. John arrived with a blanket and covered Nat up. Wellstead and Harry moved away in quiet conversation, then the Captain spoke loudly to the men.

'Nat's not in a good way. His leg's broken and he's had a nasty bump on the head. He needs a surgeon quickly. There's too much west in the wind now to fetch Poole, and Christchurch is shallow with nowhere to anchor, so we'll go into Lymington and get him to a surgeon.' There was a murmur of approval from the men at this announcement. He spoke again. 'The Needles Channel will be hard going when the tide turns, so we'll sail close inshore and through the North Channel,' adding with gentleness in his voice, 'The motion's easier in the cabin. Get Nat into my bunk, then we'll wear round. Go easy on him.'

Harry and some of the men carried Nat gently to the cabin and put him in Wellstead's bunk, while the rest of us wore the ship round and put her on a course taking her in towards the land. Despite her reduced sail, the ship heeled in the strong wind and bowled along at a good speed. On nearing the land we wore ship again and ran along the coast of low gravel cliffs, desolate and uninhabited. Eventually the coast turned into a shingle beach, like the Chesil Beach but much smaller. Wellstead told me that there were large banks called the Shingles offshore and a narrow channel close into the beach. I believed him as I could see the waves breaking furiously offshore. Despite the strong ebbing tide the ship ran fast along the beach, until we came to a castle at its end.

'Hurst Castle,' declared Wellstead, 'guards the entrance to the Solent.'

I could see for myself that the gap between Hurst Castle and the Isle of Wight was only two miles or so across. As we rounded the low shingle point on which the castle was built, we wore her round again and the *Cicely* drove through Hurst Narrows into the Solent, throwing spray aside as she tore through the overfalls created by the ebbing tide. The wind was now blowing very strongly and Wellstead decided against trying for Lymington, as it would be too rough to transfer Nat into a boat for the passage upriver, and he did not know if the ship herself could get into the river.

When we had passed through the Narrows we bore up and anchored in sheltered water at the mouth of a small creek called Keyhaven, tucked in behind the castle. Wellstead could not leave the ship while she was anchored in a gale, so he instructed the Mate to take the boat ashore with Nat and to find a surgeon. He was anxious to deplete the ship's crew as little as possible, so the shore party consisted of myself, a seaman called Jake and the Mate. I saw Wellstead giving the

Mate instructions and noticed him hand over some money in a bag. Nat was lowered into the boat on a makeshift stretcher and, with the Mate steering, we set off into the creek.

The wind was blowing strongly off the land and it was a hard row, but eventually we got in, aided by the tide which was now flooding. We had hoped that there would be boats inside the creek, perhaps ones associated with the castle, but we were disappointed. The only vessel was a ketch, swinging to her anchor, clearly deserted. I noticed her tall, heavily raked masts and long bowsprit, and with a start of recognition realised that I'd seen her before, on a dark night miles offshore, silhouetted against the horizon with a dim blue lamp burning in her shrouds. She was a free trader, a contraband runner, and as we passed astern I saw the name *True Vine* on her counter.

Dispirited, we began to row up the creek. This was easier as the curve in the channel brought the wind on the beam, but it was still hard going. In the waning light we could see a few houses in the distance. The creek had soft muddy banks and wound its way through mudflats covered in saltgrass. It was completely desolate, the only sound except for the wind the dismal calling of sea birds. Though the tide was flooding, the water was shallow and it was difficult to see where the channel was. Several times the boat ran aground and Jake and I had to clamber overboard and push the boat through the sticky mud. Jake proved himself to be a stalwart companion, strong and uncomplaining. The Mate, though, stuck to the tiller and did not offer to assist when we got on the mud. Nat lay on his stretcher, pale and unmoving.

Eventually we came to some small wharves against which fishing boats lay. We ran the boat onto a gravel beach littered with piles of fishing gear and looked about in vain for inhabitants. Eventually the Mate instructed me in a vague way to go and find help so I set off up the small road which led away from the beach. The land here seemed strange to me, with no clear divide between sea and shore. After about a quarter of a mile I came upon an inn, the Gun, and pushed open the door. The room was crowded and there was a roar of conversation, which rapidly died as the patrons noticed me. Within seconds there was complete silence and I felt many eyes on me as I walked up to the bar.

'I beg your pardon,' I said in as loud a voice as I could to the woman behind the bar. 'I'm from a ship anchored off Hurst Point. We've brought an injured shipmate ashore, fallen from the rigging, and must get him to a surgeon.' This speech was met with silence and I realised that I was an object of suspicion.

The landlady spoke at last, 'What's the name of your ship, son, and where's she from?'

I spoke with as much confidence as I could muster. 'The *Cicely*, ma'am, from Weymouth, with a cargo of stone from Portland bound for London.'

These facts were received impassively by the clientele. 'And what's your name, and where are you from?'

'Jack Stone, ma'am, from Portland, apprentice to Mr Wellstead, the *Cicely*'s owner.'

A gruff voice from behind me said, 'I knows a Jacob Stone from Portland, do you know him?'

As I answered I suddenly realised why there was such suspicion of strangers at the Gun. 'He's my father, and I guess his profession is the same as yours.' The inn's customers clearly approved of my reply as a buzz of conversation then broke out. The owner of the gruff voice, a large seafaring man, came up to me and clapped me on the back.

'Jacob Stone's boy! I can see it in your face now. How's your father? I haven't seen him for two years or more.' He thrust out his hand. 'Gabriel Merrifield, ketch *True Vine*, at your service.' As he shook my hand he added in a lowered voice, 'Sorry for the reception just then, but the preventative spies are everywhere.'

I replied, 'My father's fine, thank you, sir. I'm not a spy, but I must get my shipmate to a doctor quickly.'

'There's a doctor at Milford, couple of miles away. Can he walk?'

'No, sir, he's unconscious and his leg's broke. He's very sick.'

Merrifield became decisive and spoke in a commanding tone. 'Lads, there's an injured sailor at Keyhaven hard needs to be taken to the surgeon. Get the cart and we'll push him there.' That Merrifield knew where there was a surgeon and had a cart to take him there with was good news indeed, and I was thankful that luck had brought me to this place on the coast where my father was known.

I left the inn with Merrifield and we walked down to the beach. As I introduced him to my shipmates, the cart, which had two large wheels, arrived propelled by several men. We loaded Nat on his plank into the cart and lashed the plank in place. There was a good deal of straw already in the cart and we laid Nat's pallet on this, hoping that it would give him a softer ride.

Nat looked very ill, the journey was doing him no good at all. He occasionally moved his limbs, but his face was deadly white, except for two angry looking spots of red on his cheeks. Merrifield looked at him. 'Fever's coming, let's get him to the doc's quick.'

The men pushed the cart up the road. As we drew level with the Gun, the Mate said to nobody in particular, 'You don't need me. I'm going inside here in case Wellstead sends ashore for us. This is the first place they'll look.' Merrifield gave him a surprised look but said nothing, and Jake raised his eyebrows. I kept my counsel, as I was delighted that the Mate was not to accompany us. I had a hearty dislike of him and he frightened me.

We set off up the road towards Milford. I was glad that we had Merrifield and his men as guides, as I suspected they knew the road well and were used to operating in the dark without lights. After a mile or so of brisk progress we drew level with some bushes, and there was a shout.

'In the King's name, stop or we'll fire. Put your hands on your heads and stand fast!'

Merrifield's voice rang out, 'Do as he says, lads. Is that you, Lieutenant Rudd?'

'It is, Merrifield. I believe I have you now.' I heard the sound of lanterns being lit and a tall thin officer stepped forward and addressed Merrifield. The two clearly knew each other. The officer spoke again. 'Can you explain your presence here with this cart?'

'Indeed I can', came the reply. 'We're assisting this young man here to take his injured shipmate to the surgeon in Milford.'

There was a snort of disbelief in reply and more Revenue men stepped forward into the light, their muskets trained on Merrifield and his men. There were a lot of them, probably thirty or so, and I expected that there were others concealed at the side of the road. Despite this the men were clearly nervous and I expect that most of them would rather have been in their beds. The Lieutenant, however, did not seem to be troubled by self-doubt as he addressed our party. He waved his pistol at a spot in the road.

'Move over there and lie down.' He was a stooped man of about fifty, dressed in the blue and red uniform of his service. We had no option but to comply, and lay on the cold road, the muskets of the King's men covering us.

The Lieutenant turned back to the cart. 'You there, on the cart, didn't you hear me? Get over here immediately.' Nat did not stir, and the Lieutenant's voice became more excited. 'I said get off the cart!'

He moved forward and pulled the blanket back from Nat's face, repeating 'Get off the cart!' Nat still did not move and the Lieutenant seemed to consider this an affront to his authority. In a jerky and agitated manner he put his pistol against Nat's head.

'Move, I said, or I'll blow your brains out.'

I was very frightened by this time and blurted out without

55

thinking, 'He's bad hurt, sir, fell from the rigging, and he'll die unless we get him to a surgeon quick.'

Without turning the Lieutenant spoke, his voice angry, 'Don't you think I can see through your childish tricks? I've got you red-handed this time.'

He addressed the unmoving figure of Nat. 'I'll count to five and then I'll fire. Move!'

Merrifield spoke, his gruff voice calm. 'Lieutenant Rudd, sir, the man really is hurt. He's not from my ship, we ....'

He was interrupted by the Lieutenant. 'You heard what I said. One!' Rudd's voice was high and trembling. 'Two!'

I could not bear what was happening. I had been brought up on stories of the preventative service's brutality and believed them capable of anything. I was sure that Nat would be murdered by the Lieutenant. I started to get up from the road, but the boot of one of the King's men pushed me back down. I watched horrified as Rudd called out 'Three!'

At that moment, the sergeant, a large black-bearded man, stepped forward. He laid one hand on the Lieutenant's arm and with the other guided the pistol so that it was pointing at the ground. Relief flooded over me. The sergeant spoke, his voice respectful and calm.

'Sir, if you fire your pistol you'll rouse every smuggler for miles around and we'll have a battle on our hands, with respect, sir.'

The Lieutenant shook his head as though emerging from a dream. 'Oh, very good sergeant, you're quite right, yes of course. We know what the people are like around here, best get them to Lymington straight away.' As he spoke, the sergeant had been holding up his lantern and looking closely at Nat.

'Sir, I think this man's really sick, he don't look too good to me. Perhaps we could just rummage underneath him, it's very bad to move a sick man too much.'

The Lieutenant seemed to have lost interest and took a step back from the cart. 'Yes, very well sergeant, you may be right. Search underneath the man without moving him too much.'

This concern about Nat's comfort, from a man who had been about to blow his brains out a minute or so ago, astonished me. It would not do so now, as I have had great experience of how some men are affected by responsibility and the stress of action.

The sergeant beckoned to two of his men, who came forward and felt around in the straw under Nat's pallet. The search was thorough and took several minutes.

'Nothing here,' declared the man.

Without waiting for an order, we saw the troopers covering us with their muskets put their arms up, and we got off the ground. I had the distinct impression that the preventative men were relieved that nothing had been found and the affair had ended peacefully, and this impression was reinforced when I saw the men in uniform talking to the seamen.

The Lieutenant's voice had returned to normal. 'Very well, Merrifield, you may proceed.' He turned and touched his hat. Needing no further encouragement we picked up the handles of the cart and went smartly up the road. I was too preoccupied with Nat's plight to take much notice, but there seemed considerable resentment at the Lieutenant's behaviour, and I knew that the tale would be embroidered and added to the contrabanders' stock of stories of the King's men's brutality.

I had been involved in contrabanding all my life till then and viewed the Revenue as the enemy of the honest sailor, hard pressed to make a living from the sea. Looking back, though, I must allow that the contrabanders themselves were not above reproach. They were a lawless bunch and, going about as they often did in large armed gangs, frequently terrified ordinary people, though those same people were glad enough to make use of the goods they brought in.

We arrived shortly at the village of Milford, a small place with few lights showing in the windows, and stopped outside a larger house which I was assured was the residence of the surgeon. We knocked on the door, a curtain was drawn back and the door quickly opened by a tall thin man, who I assumed was the doctor. I guessed that opening the door meant that the occupant was familiar with Merrifield and his men, because we could not have looked very prepossessing, especially with our clothes covered in mud from our time lying on the road.

As soon as the doctor saw Nat he quickly moved to his side, felt his brow and opened an eyelid. He lifted the blanket and saw the misshapen leg.

'What's happened?' he asked.

'Fell out of the rigging on this lad's ship,' replied Merrifield, pointing to me.

'Get him inside, but be gentle,' said the doctor. 'Lay the stretcher on the table in the front room.' As the men carried Nat into the house, the doctor turned to me.

'Tell me what you know. Has he spoken since he fell? Have you given him anything?'

Quickly I told him what he wanted to know, and he walked away from me and into the room with Nat, rolling up his sleeves as he did so. I heard activity in the back of the house and assumed that the doctor's wife or servant was coming to assist.

A few minutes later Merrifield and the men came out to where I was waiting by the door. Merrifield spoke, 'Doctor says his leg's broke bad, but he can put it in a splint and it'll fix. Bump on the head's more worrying, but he thinks he'll recover. He's given him some laudanum and he's easier. Doctor'll work on him, and in the morning he'll have him taken over to Betty Atkinson's house where he can lie quiet. When you come back from London, you can pick him up.'

This came as wonderful relief to me and probably to Jake as well, who was amply living up to his reputation aboard the *Cicely* as a man of few words. We walked back to the Gun Inn with the men pushing the empty cart, Merrifield asking many questions about my father and the *Cicely*. He told me about his ketch.

'Fastest craft for miles, she is, but the trade's very down now, what with the war, and the Revenue's active as well. There's even talk of building coastguard cottages on Hurst Spit.'

As we neared Keyhaven, a thought struck me. 'There'll be doctor's bills and lodging to pay for Nat, but I saw the skipper give the Mate money before we came ashore.'

Merrifield nodded in approval. 'He sounds a good man, your skipper.'

We went inside the Gun, and the men wasted no time in relaying our story. We were given food and drink, which I was sorely in need of by this time, and after I had eaten felt better. Jake, who was sitting opposite me, was looking concerned.

'We should be getting back to the ship, but I think there may be some difficulty.'

As he spoke he inclined his head towards a table in the corner of the inn and to my horror I saw the Mate slumped forward, a bottle and glass on the table in front of him. At that moment Merrifield came up to us.

'Your Mate's dead drunk,' he said with contempt in his voice. 'You were saying about the money?'

Jake and I walked over to the Mate's table. Jake shook him gently by the shoulder.

'Excuse me, sir, it's time to go back to the ship.' There was no response, so Jake shook him a little harder. The Mate lifted his eyes, focusing slowly on Jake.

'What do you want?'

'Time to go back to the ship, sir,' repeated Jake.

The Mate made no response, but his eyes wandered over to where I was standing.

'Oh, it's the Captain's little spy,' he said with a slurred sneer, 'such a shame you didn't drown. I wouldn't have bothered going back for you, not worth stopping the ship for a smuggling fisherboy.'

This was perhaps an ill-judged remark to make in the Gun, whose clientele was largely drawn from the ranks of fishermen and smugglers. Merrifield and two of his men drew near to the table. Merrifield spoke.

'I've been given to understand that the Captain of your ship gave you some money for the upkeep of that poor sailor. If you give it to me I'll make sure it's taken up to the doctor and Betty Atkinson first thing tomorrow morning.'

The Mate looked up at him. 'I don't have any money, who told you I did? That lying little fisherboy, I'll be bound.' The repeated disparaging reference to the fishing profession was not well received by the inn's customers.

'He's spent a pile of money in here this evening,' spoke up one of them.

'That he has,' interjected the landlady, 'best food and wine.'

Merrifield eyed him with suspicion. 'Whose money have you been spending?' There was a menacing note in his voice.

The Mate seemed suddenly to recognise his predicament and his tone became pleading, much as it had done that night in Wapping.

'My own, of course. Captain didn't give me any money. He's a well-known liar, that boy.'

'He's not, he's a good lad,' interjected Jake, to my surprise.

Merrifield spoke again, his tone decisive. 'Hand the money over, Mr Mate.'

The Mate should have realised the game was up then, but he was too far gone in drink. What happened next amazed me. Merrifield nodded to two of his men who moved to either side of the Mate and quickly pushed him to the ground. They grabbed one leg each and held the Mate upside down off the floor. As they did so a bag with some coins fell out of his clothes and Merrifield bent and picked it up. There was general laughter from the customers and a flurry of coins fell on the floor around the Mate's head, thrown by the landlady.

'I'm not taking any money that's been stolen from a poor sailor by you,' she said to the Mate in a loud voice, and Merrifield nodded to her and scooped the coins off the floor. There was a general murmur of approval for the landlady from the customers.

Merrifield spoke to his men. 'Put him down now,' and the men dropped the Mate with a bump onto the floor, where he stayed. Merrifield asked the landlady for paper and pen and wrote out a receipt for the money, which he gave to Jake.

'Give that to your Captain, and tell him he's welcome aboard my ketch whenever we might meet.'

The Mate, who seemed to have lapsed into a drunken stupor, was carried down to the boat in the cart and dumped unceremoniously in the bottom of the boat. By the time we got back to the *Cicely* the gale had passed and a north-westerly breeze was blowing under a starry sky. We were seen approaching the ship, and Wellstead was at the rail as we arrived. The Mate, who had recovered somewhat, slunk off into his berth. Wellstead took Jake and I into the cabin and listened to our account of what had happened, occasionally asking questions to prompt us. His eyes narrowed when he heard of the Mate's behaviour, but he made no comment, taking Merrifield's receipt and putting it in a drawer.

He spoke when we had finished. 'You've done well, it seems as though Nat is in good hands. We'll come back for him when we're homeward bound. We'll get underway now. I don't want to be going past Spithead in daylight if we can avoid it.' Spithead is the name for the strip of water between Portsmouth and the Isle of Wight where the Royal Navy has its main anchorage, and Wellstead was expressing the merchant seaman's fear of the press gang. 'Seems you've had one lucky escape from serving in the Navy already,' he continued, aware that recently smugglers caught by the preventative men had been pressed into service in the Navy.

We weighed anchor, not an easy task as it had been well dug into the seabed by the gale, and made good speed up the Solent, passing near the fleet in the dark without incident or challenge. Two days later we were back at anchor at the Nore, waiting for the morning tide to take us to our berth in Wapping.

Chapter 8
Boarded!

Wapping had not changed much since our last visit, but my experience as a member of the *Cicely's* crew seemed to have matured me. Wellstead must have appreciated this because I was no longer confined to the ship and was sometimes given errands to run, though I was not allowed to accompany the crew on their runs ashore. Since the incident at Keyhaven the Mate had almost given up the pretence of being part of the ship's company. I now realise that he was firmly in opium's terrible grip and that he took to drink when he could not get opium. Every imaginable vice, including opium, was to be had at Wapping, and on our first night alongside I watched as he slipped off ashore. I was so afraid of being on the ship with him alone that I decided I would find a good place to hide and stay in it until the crew returned.

Wellstead was a considerate man and gave much thought to improving the efficiency of the ship. As a consequence the *Cicely* was blessed with equipment and gadgets uncommon on a ship of her type. Most of these were useful, but occasionally Wellstead made some improvement which the sailors, who were a conservative breed, tried their best not to use. An advance that fell into this category were nets which could be used for slinging irregularly shaped cargo. The nets had not been used since I was aboard and were kept in a large bin at the rail near the stern. The bin had become part of the furniture of the ship and was frequently used as a seat or workbench. Wellstead was very protective of his nets, and would not allow anything else to be put into the bin. I think he felt that their hour would come, and his purchase of them would be vindicated. I got into the bin, wedging the top open slightly with a piece of wood. Though it was cramped and somewhat lumpy I thought it would be an acceptable spot for a couple of hours until the crew returned, and settled down to wait. It must have been comfortable because I was woken some hours later by the straggling arrival of the crew. I got gratefully into my bunk, as the net bin had left me feeling somewhat sore.

Our stay in London was uneventful. Wellstead took me once more into the city, and I ran several errands to the agent in Leadenhall Street. As before, when we finished discharging the hay we went upriver to the stone wharf. Wellstead secured a cargo of roundshot for Portsmouth, and we loaded this at a berth at the great arsenal of Woolwich.

August was nearly over by the time we made our way down the river, passing the fleet anchored at the Nore. At noon on the following day we passed the South Foreland and entered the Channel. Nat's absence had made us a man short, and as a substitute I was put into the Mate's watch. When we relieved the Port watch at midnight the ship was about ten miles south of Littlehampton. The Sussex coast is low there, we could not see the land to the north of us, and the high bulk of the Isle of Wight was not yet visible. A moderate northerly breeze was blowing and this meant that the sea was slight, as the distance between the ship and the land was not great enough for large waves to build up. The moon, shining from a clear sky, sparkled on the sea, and gave some light.

The Mate was showing an unusually keen interest in the navigation of the ship and several times went into the cabin to check the chart, calling out course corrections to the helmsman after each visit. We could see the lights of other ships going down Channel nearby, and occasionally the lights of ships going in the opposite direction would appear and then pass quickly. Sometimes a ship would come close enough to enable us to make out her shape in the moonlight, but generally we saw only the lights. Wellstead was very keen that a good lookout should be kept, and on his watch a man was permanently posted either in the bow or aloft. I am sure that he had instructed the Mate to follow the same procedure, but on that night in the Channel the Starboard watch kept no lookout.

At one o'clock the ship was running about six knots. With the moderate steady breeze there was not much for us to do, and one of the men had gone into the galley to make tea for the watch. Except for the helmsman, the men were gathered near the door, making helpful comments to the man in the galley and waiting for their tea. I was on the poop deck, leaning against the rail and enjoying the sensation of the *Cicely* running well, when I noticed a ship displaying three vertical lights about a mile away on the starboard bow. I did not take much notice, but when I looked up a few minutes later the lights were closer and seemed to be on the same bearing, which meant a collision course, a fairly common occurrence in the busy Channel. I looked towards the wheel, but lost interest when I saw that the Mate had noticed the other ship and was following its progress closely.

When I next looked the other ship was so close that I could make out her shape, a rakish cutter of fifty tons or so, built for speed and heavily canvassed. She was heeled over and I could see the foaming bow wave and her sails straining at the sheets. The lights in the rigging were extinguished as I watched and on her deck I could make out indistinct figures moving around.

From that moment things happened very quickly. I heard a shouted order and the crash and thunder of the cutter's sails, and saw her gybe and surge up alongside us, heeling wildly. It was an amazing display of seamanship, but not one I could appreciate, for with sudden insight I realised the full horror of what was happening. We were about to be boarded. As the hulls came into contact I heard a loud thud and splintering noises, and I staggered as the impact rocked the *Cicely*. Lesser breaking noises came from above as the spars and rigging of the two vessels became locked in a tangled embrace. I saw men on the deck of the cutter, and grapnels being thrown which caught in the bulwarks of our ship. Suddenly men were climbing over the *Cicely*'s side, barefoot sailors literally armed to the teeth, seemingly covered all over with cutlasses, pistols and axes. They did not look about them when they got on board, but went confidently about their business with frightening, well drilled efficiency.

I crouched down behind the net bin, from where I had a view of the main deck, and watched as the boarders split into several groups, the man who seemed to be the leader shouting, 'In the name of the King, stand where you are,' as he rushed towards the wheel, accompanied by several heavily armed men. Another group brandishing pistols and cutlasses ran towards the galley, where my watchmates stood transfixed, and a third group went into the fo'c'stle. As the boarders reached the wheel I realised with a start that they were led by the man with the scarred head. He was wearing a naval uniform and carried a pistol in his left hand and a cutlass in his right. As he approached, the helmsman, without being told, took his hands off the wheel and raised them above his head. One of the boarders pushed him aside and took the wheel himself.

That the ship had been boarded by a party led by the man with the scarred head was staggering, but I was shocked even more by what happened next. Wellstead came bursting out of the cabin door, his coat unbuttoned and shouting, 'What's going on, what've we hit?' only to stop short when he saw the man with the scarred head pointing his pistol at him. With his jaw open in astonishment, he looked the man in the face and said, 'Who are you? What are you doing here?'

The man spoke, his English perfect and only slightly accented. 'Captain Morlaix, of the Republican Navy. The Republic has need of your ship, Captain Wellstead.' Two French sailors grabbed Wellstead as Morlaix spoke and, with his shoulders slumped, dragged him forwards, joining the remainder of the *Cicely*'s crew who were sitting disconsolately by the fo'c'stle. French sailors moved among the men, tying their hands in front of them.

Orders were given in French, and I watched in dismay as the crew was herded over the bulwark onto the deck of the cutter and then moved below into her hold. As they went, I saw one of the French sailors pointing to a swivel trained on the hatch and knew that he was explaining to the crew that any attempt at escape would end in a bloody discharge of grapeshot. One of the crew, I could not see who it was, started shouting in a hysterical way. I think that he was overcome by the prospect of being locked in the hold. His cries were cut short by a blow from Harry, who undoubtedly realised that any show of resistance was extremely dangerous, given the nervousness of the French sailors in their hazardous undertaking. The hatch and the French crew started preparations for separating the two vessels. At that moment the Mate walked out of the cabin onto the deck, swaying slightly, and stood with his attention held by the scene on the cutter. For a second I thought that he also had been overlooked by the French, but then I noticed a pistol stuck into his belt and realised that he was in league with them.

He was joined by Morlaix, who was giving orders to the sailors in rapid French. It is the fashion nowadays to disparage the French Navy, and it is true that they were decidedly inferior to the Royal Navy in big ship actions, but the effectiveness of their privateers in later years should not be forgotten. In any event, in all my years at sea I have never seen an operation carried out with such calm efficiency as the one that night by Morlaix and his men, and it was a foretaste of things to come.

Morlaix turned to the Mate and there was anger in his voice. 'You've been drinking!'

I heard the Mate reply, 'To celebrate our success and my new-found riches.' He waved his arms expansively.

Morlaix spoke, his voice firm. 'We have not succeeded, and you're not rich yet. This was the easy part. We've got to get the ship to France, and you won't be able to help do that if you're drunk.' His tone became more conciliatory. 'Let us get the ship underway, and then we will have some food.'

I was thoroughly terrified by this time. The Mate was frightening enough in normal circumstances, but the thought of him in league with the French, drunk and wandering the ship with a pistol in his belt turned me into a trembling wreck. If I was caught I would be killed! I sunk down as far as I could behind the net bin, just about all in, with nowhere to run to. There were crashes and shouts as the cutter separated from the *Cicely*. Hoping that this would distract the French, I opened the lid of the bin, which felt heavy as lead to my fear-weakened muscles. I got inside, let the lid shut over me and burrowed down as much as I could under the nets.

I waited in fear for the lid to be wrenched open, but as the minutes passed I realised that I had not been seen, and my trembling abated. I heard more orders given in French and felt the *Cicely* come upright as the wind was brought onto the quarter. I knew that this meant that she was heading south-west, towards France. I was utterly exhausted, drained of all energy, and I do not believe that at that moment I could have moved myself even if the ship had sunk.

***

When I awoke, the inside of the bin was lit by sunlight leaking round the edges of the lid, which was not very tight fitting. I was stiff and sore, and as I remembered the events of the night before, a feeling of unreality came over me. Was the ship really in the hands of the French, led by the scar-headed man, assisted by the Mate? It seemed impossible, but through the walls of the bin I heard an order given in French and I knew beyond doubt that my memories were true.

I tried to estimate how long I had been asleep. The sun was not shining directly into the gaps between the box and the lid, so it was not low on the horizon and the top of the box felt warm to my touch. I guessed that it was late morning or early afternoon, which meant that I had been asleep for ten or twelve hours. The ship was heeling to the wind, on the starboard tack. Her motion suggested to me that she was close hauled. Gusts of wind blew through the gaps in the lid and I realised that if the ship was still heading south-west, the wind was now westerly and quite strong.

The feeling of unreality was fostered by the sounds and motion of the ship, so familiar to me. I could hear the life of the ship and feel it, but I could take no part in it. I felt like a ghost haunting the house of its childhood, now inhabited by another generation. What could I do? There seemed to be no obvious answer. I dearly wished I had been captured with my shipmates and was with them in the hold of the cutter. I considered giving myself up, but the thought of the Mate in league with the French persuaded me against that course of action. For the moment, all I could think of doing was to stay hidden.

For some time I had been aware of activity on the deck, with orders being given and the ship coming more upright as sail was taken in. I realised that something was going on, and with pounding heart I raised my head and cracked open the lid of the bin. For a moment the light blinded me, but I was relieved when I saw that the deck round me was deserted. I slipped the wooden wedge into the gap, and watched as a warship appeared to weather of us. She was a small frigate, flying a large British ensign, with signal flags fluttering from her mizzen. She was close to the *Cicely* and rapidly overhauling us. I watched as she drew level with us and reduced sail smartly to match our speed. Simultaneously the upper gunports opened and I saw the black muzzles of guns emerge. I realised that I was watching the British blockade of France in operation, and a surge of hope ran through me.

The warship was very close, perhaps fifty yards away. I saw an officer on the quarterdeck raise a speaking trumpet to his mouth and shout slowly and distinctly, 'What ship? What is your home port?'

I heard the Mate answer, his voice steady, '*Cicely*, Weymouth.'

The warship's officer brought his speaking trumpet up again. 'Where are you from, where are you bound, and what is your cargo?'

The Mate replied again, 'London, for Jersey, general cargo including garrison stores.'

There was a pause while this information was considered, and probably checked against documents carried by the warship. I was in a ferment of anxiety. What should I do? If the warship boarded us I might be saved, but if I tried to attract the Navy's attention the Frenchmen would surely kill me. Could I shout and jump overboard, trusting to be noticed and rescued? The sea was rough, and after my experience in the North Sea I knew that it was likely that once overboard I would never be found.

I realised that if the warship sent a boarding party to the *Cicely* it would be surprised by fierce armed resistance and would no doubt be repulsed, which would lead to the deaths of many of my countrymen, and probably myself when the *Cicely* was sunk by the frigate's guns.

In the event, I did nothing. No boarding party was sent, and I did not engage in any heroics. The officer on the frigate shouted, 'Very well, *Cicely*, proceed. *Bon voyage*.' The moment was lost. I watched despondent as the frigate's guns were pulled back in and the ports closed. Men ran on her deck and she tacked away from the *Cicely*. As she rounded up into the wind I saw the name *Waterwitch* on her stern. She settled onto the other tack, sail was crowded on, and in a few minutes she was an indistinct speck. My chance had gone and I felt sick at my lack of courage. I should have done something, but I hadn't. I lay back into the nets, exhausted, and felt the *Cicely* heel once more to the wind.

Gradually depression gave way to the optimism of youth

and I began to think about what was happening. The Mate had told the warship that the *Cicely* was headed for Jersey, and the *Waterwitch's* officers had believed him. I had not before thought of the status of the Channel Islands, but I now realised that they must be in English hands. For the Mate to be believed, the *Cicely* must have been on a course towards Jersey, and this meant that she must be making for a French port near the island. I had only a vague idea of the shape of the French coast and the relative position of the Channel Islands. I tried to visualise Wellstead's chart. There was a peninsular with Cherbourg at its tip and the Channel Islands off its western side, but the details were very hazy in my mind.

The ship was pitching quite heavily now and I could hear the crashing of waves. After an hour or so I risked another look out of the bin but could see nothing except a confused seascape. From the look of the sea I realised that the tidal stream must be strong. Some time later I felt sail being reduced, and the sea became calmer. There was much shouting and running around, at times only inches from my hiding place. Though the language of the sailors was strange to me, I realised that the ship was being brought into port and tied up alongside a wharf. We had arrived in France!

Activity on the ship gradually died away. I heard people talking and laughing and realised that the sailors were going ashore, cheerful in the knowledge that their difficult task had been accomplished. Eventually there was complete silence, and after waiting for half an hour or so I raised the cover of the bin enough to look around.

The ship was in port, but it was not like the bustling ports I was accustomed to and, indeed, gave the impression of being deserted. There was a rough wharf and one or two small unlit wooden buildings, but there were no other ships nearby. As I looked round, there was another difference between this port and the others the *Cicely* had visited. This one had no water. The ship's keel was resting on the dry sandy bed of an estuary. A trickle of water could be seen in the centre of the bed, and I could make out a line of breakers about a mile away to seaward, but the *Cicely* was high and dry. To one accustomed to the moderate rise and fall of the tides along England's southern shore, the tidal range of thirty feet or more in the Channel Islands and the adjacent French coast comes as a surprise. It brings, literally, a new dimension to seafaring. At low tides, especially spring tides, miles of seabed are uncovered, and rocks which at high tide were awash become miniature mountains above a sandy plain.

I decided that I must get out of the bin. I was cramped and aching and had two desperate needs – food and water, and to relieve a bladder aching beyond endurance. I just could not stay where I was. I opened the lid of the bin and climbed out. Such were the aches in my body that I had difficulty in rising, but I managed to stand still long enough to ensure that there was nobody about, and then to move to the rail and add my own contribution to the trickle of water in the estuary bed. My legs felt very weak, so I sat on the grating by the wheel and looked around. Upriver I could see a small town, huddled by a quay crowded with the masts of fishing boats, and in the other direction waves breaking on the bar at the mouth of the estuary. The land in the vicinity of the *Cicely*'s berth was flat for several hundred yards and was bordered by a steep hill covered in low trees and gorse. France!

Chapter 9
Cap de Carteret

I was weak from hunger and thirst, and knew that even at the risk of capture I had to find food and drink. To go to the galley meant walking the entire length of the moonlit deck, and I decided to look first in the cabin, as I knew Wellstead kept food there to eat on occasions when the galley was not manned.

Slowly, for my body ached terribly, I climbed off the poop deck and tried the cabin door handle. To my relief it turned easily and I pushed the door open slowly. As my eyes became accustomed to the gloom I saw the remains of a meal on the table. With my mouth watering I walked over to it and quickly grabbed some bread and a large bottle which turned out to contain beer. Carrying my hoard, I moved back up to the poop deck and sat in the shadows of the net bin to consume my meal.

I drank long and deep from the beer and ate all the bread. When it was finished I realised that I was still hungry, and in my mind's eye I saw the cheese I had left on the cabin table. I don't know if I was emboldened by the beer, but I decided that I must have that cheese, and set out once more for the cabin. I went into the room as before, but as I went through the door I noticed one of Wellstead's coats hanging up. As the night had become chilly I took it from its hook and put it on. The coat was a long one, dark blue in colour and much too big for me. It had deep pockets and I filled these with the remains of the meal on the table, grabbing the food indiscriminately. On an impulse, I took a knife off the table and slipped it into a pocket with the food. The familiar surroundings of the cabin reassured me, and I opened the cabin door with less caution than I should have.

I was brought back to reality when I saw the Mate get off the end of the steeply sloping gangway and start to walk along the moonlit deck towards the cabin. I shrank back inside the doorway, hoping that he would not see me, but my hope was dashed when he stopped in surprise, shouted in rage and started towards me, pulling at the pistol in his belt. I realised that I could not hide in the cabin or anywhere else on the ship and that my only chance was to get ashore. Better to be caught by the French than by the Mate, who hated me and would surely kill me if he could. He was between me and the gangway, and I ran towards him as fast as I could, intending to swerve round him. As I neared him he suddenly lunged towards me and we collided. The impact knocked the breath out of me, but I stayed on my feet. My sudden move, however, had surprised him, and he fell onto the deck, cursing.

'Get away, get away' was all I could think and I ran helter-skelter up the gangway. There was a step where it went onto the wharf, only a matter of a few inches, but it was enough to trip me in my weakened state and I fell heavily. I thought, 'What a way to arrive in France!' and started to get to my feet but was stopped by an excruciating pain in my ankle. I had injured it somehow.

I knelt on the wharf, rubbing my ankle, and looked back towards the ship. The Mate appeared at the bottom of the gangway, pistol in hand. I seemed to lose the power of movement, like a bird mesmerised by a snake. Perhaps twenty feet separated us and I could clearly see the smile of satisfaction on his face as he raised the pistol and deliberately pointed it at me, the dark circle of the muzzle wavering slightly in his hand. I saw his finger tighten on the trigger and there was a flash, but just a flash and no bang. The pistol had misfired. Pain or no pain, I got to my feet and staggered off towards the hill. My intention had been to climb up the hill and hide in the furze, but when I got across the flat ground I realised that it was too steep to climb with my hurt ankle.

I looked round and saw the Mate go down the gangway and start after me. He realised I was limping and stopped to reload his pistol. I ran along the base of the hill, towards the sea, looking for a way up. I had gone a few hundred yards and was nearly at the beach when I came to a rough path leading upwards. I looked back and saw the Mate close behind me, pistol in hand. There was no choice. I started up the path as quickly as I could, faint with the pain from my ankle. The track was narrow, cut by passing feet into the rough grass of the hillside. The soil was thin and sandy and there were occasional outcrops of rock, which made the going very rough. Fear drove me, and I scrambled up the hill, tripping over the rocks and being scratched by the gorse bushes and brambles which overhung the track. I did not look round but could hear the Mate behind me, frighteningly close. I came to a fork in the path and hesitated, and at that moment I heard, seemingly almost in my ears, the bang of the pistol.

And that was it, the bang, no pain, nothing – he'd missed. My contrabanding youth had given me some experience of being under fire, and I realised that I hadn't even heard the noise of the ball, so he must have shot very wild.

I had started to scramble up the path again, the pain in my ankle severe, when I felt a terrific blow on my back, which made me stagger so that my hands touched the ground. I turned to see the cause of the blow and saw the Mate's pistol lying on the path. He had thrown it at me, and without thinking I picked it up and threw it as far away as I could. I looked up and saw him standing a few yards away, breathing heavily. He made no move towards me, and I crouched down, facing him, digging my fingers into the sandy soil. In the moonlight he was a terrifying figure, his chest heaving and his eyes fixed on me with a look of hatred. I believe by this time he was beyond rational thought, tipped into madness by his craving for opium and the reflection of his treason.

He spoke, his voice rasping from his throat. 'So, it's the little fisherboy, the Captain's spy. Is your leg hurt, and your back?

Don't worry, your pains won't be troubling you much longer.' He laughed, a horrible grating noise. 'If only Wellstead could see me now. He'd see who was the better man. I've come out on top, and he'd understand that. He's finished, hopeless, in a French dungeon by now. I'm rich now you know. Rich. The French have paid me well, and there's more to come. They paid me for getting the ship for them, straightaway, as soon as we arrived at Carteret, and there'll be more when we get into Weymouth and get the King.'

He looked at me, his head cocked to one side.

'Surprised are you? Kneeling there with your mouth hanging open? The Mate of the *Cicely* so important to the operation? Oh yes, Morlaix realised my value, not like Wellstead. He's a good judge of men, Morlaix is.'

All I wanted was to get away from this madman, but he seemed determined to talk to me. I listened, alert for any move on his part, but I was gradually recovering my breath, rocking slightly from side to side to stop my leg muscles freezing up, and at the same time digging my hands into the soil.

He became calmer. 'I can see you don't believe me. Well, it's true. Morlaix and I are going to sail the *Cicely* crammed with Frenchies right into Weymouth Bay and capture the King, the frigates will be blown to bits, and after the invasion I'll be rich. That'll show Wellstead.'

I listened, but at the same time I was beginning to realise that he had underestimated me. Though he was a full-grown man and larger than me, he was not hardened as I was by the constant physical exercise of work on the ship. He had had two easy chances to kill me but had missed both of them. My nerves steadied a bit. Keep talking, I thought, I'm not dead yet, and crouched, waiting for the attack, my hands now well into the soil.

He paused. 'But you, fisherboy, you won't be around to see any of this. You're always hanging about. I know Wellstead used you to spy on me, so he could get an excuse to go to my father and get me off the ship. I nearly had you in the

North Sea, but there's no Wellstead to rescue you now.' He stopped talking and grinned horribly. I saw his muscles tense and suddenly he was rushing forward with his hands in front of him, reaching out for me, grinning. I had been waiting for this and was ready. I pulled my hands out of the cold ground, hands full of sandy soil, and, with as much force as I could muster, threw the soil at the Mate's face. My aim was good and he checked his charge, letting out a shriek of rage as his hands went to his eyes. I turned away from him and ran as fast as I could along the left fork of the path.

I went for a hundred yards or so, with the Mate gaining on me. At the crest of the hill I suddenly felt the force of the wind, salt smelling and damp, and realised that the hill was a cape jutting out into the sea. In the moonlight I saw the waves below me and ahead a huge sandy beach fringed with surf. The path was now running across a steep slope, almost a cliff, following the shoreline. About fifty feet below the path the slope became a vertical rockface, and I could hear the sea pounding on the boulders and felt the spindrift on my face. Ahead the path turned to the right and I could see some straggling gorse bushes on the landward side. I knew that the Mate would catch me soon, and as I ran I formed a desperate plan. Despite the pain in my ankle I redoubled my efforts, and when I reached the bend I had slightly increased the distance between myself and my enemy.

As soon as I turned the corner I stopped and crouched as low as I could behind the inadequate shelter of a gorse bush, taking the knife from the pocket of Wellstead's coat. It was an ordinary table knife with a bone handle, but quite sharp. Not much of a weapon, but it was all I had, and I could run no more. I grasped it firmly in both hands. By this time I had lost some of my fear of the Mate. He had shot at me twice and failed to hit me on both occasions, and he had then lost a considerable advantage by throwing the pistol at me. I knew that he was fallible.

Within seconds, the Mate reached the corner. He must have

known that he was close to catching me and he was running as hard as he could, his breath coming in great gasps. He was two or three yards away from my hiding place when he saw me, but it was too late for him to stop.

He shouted, 'I can see you', as though we were children playing hide and seek, and then he was upon me. I stood up quickly and he flinched, his hands going to his eyes, probably thinking I was going to repeat the soil-throwing trick. As he did so I drove the knife upwards as hard as I could, aiming for his stomach. I missed, but the knife went into his thigh, quite deep. There was an awful yell and he looked at me, his mouth round with surprise.

'You – you've stabbed me!' he said in a shocked tone. He took a step backwards onto the loose stones of the slope and his injured leg collapsed. He fell heavily onto his back, and rolled head over heels until he was sliding feet first on his stomach down the slope, accompanied by a miniature avalanche of stones. For a moment he hung at the edge of the cliff, his hands clawing at the ground, and then fell screaming onto the rocks below.

***

Perhaps I should have felt elated at the destruction of my enemy, but I did not. I felt drained and ashamed. I had just killed a man. I sat down with my head in my hands, and not knowing what to do recited the Lord's Prayer. 'Forgive us our trespasses.' I have never before or since felt so dejected, alone and frightened as I did that night on the windy Cap de Carteret. Even now, half a lifetime later, the thought of it makes me shudder. I forced myself to my feet and walked along the path, away from the port, away from the *Cicely*, towards I knew not what.

Before I had gone many yards I realised that the Mate would be missed in the morning and a search instigated. If his body was found in the sea it would probably be assumed that he had met with an accident while drunk, but the evidence that his end had not been entirely accidental could be seen where the fight had taken place. I forced myself to walk back to the bushes, break off a branch of furze and use it to sweep sand over the drops of blood from the Mate's wound.

When I had finished I threw the branch well off the path and continued walking. Eventually the path led away from the clifftop and emerged on a level grassy area, in the middle of which was a small ruined building, probably a chapel of some sort. Surrounding the grass were bushes about six feet tall, bent and gnarled by the prevailing wind. Ahead of me in the moonlight was the immense beach I had seen from the top of the cape, stretching out into the distance, fringed with crashing surf and bordered on the landward side by huge sand dunes. I could go no further. I crept into the bushes, pulled Wellstead's coat about me and slept.

***

When I awoke the sun was shining brightly, high in the sky, filtering between the green branches overhead. Birds were singing and I could hear the small scurrying of animals nearby. I lay on my back, still wrapped in Wellstead's great coat, remembering the awful events of the night before. I felt surprisingly healthy, refreshed by my long sleep.

My reverie was interrupted by the sound of voices, and I realised that I had been woken by people nearby. I turned over onto my front as stealthily as I could and peered cautiously out through the shrubs. I suppose that I should not have been surprised by what I saw, given the events of the night before, but it came as a shock when I saw that the clearing round the chapel contained about twenty men in an unfamiliar uniform, carrying long muskets. The men were being addressed by an officer or sergeant, I could not tell which, who was speaking rapidly and pointing with his hands. I could not understand what was being said, but it was obvious from the demeanour

78

of the group that a search for the Mate was to be undertaken and that the duties of the men were being detailed.

There was no possibility of me withdrawing further without being discovered, for the bushes became thick and brambly behind me, and so I slowly pulled Wellstead's coat over my head, lay still and fervently wished that I had never left home. My concealment was effective, for I was not noticed, and indeed I think that I was probably invisible to any but a determined searcher actually entering the bushes near me. I lay still for about half an hour until I heard the activity round the chapel subside and the men move off. I thought of moving away, but it seemed to me that I was better off staying where I was. Though the French did not know of my presence, they would be likely to question anybody found wandering that day on Cap de Carteret.

When I next looked out the clearing was deserted. I felt very hungry and suddenly remembered the food I had stowed away in the pockets of Wellstead's coat. I sat up and pulled out bread and some cheese. I thought that Wellstead must have bought the cheese in Weymouth, and the thought of this brought a great wave of melancholy over me. I was feeling sorry for myself and I am afraid that my thoughts were rather selfish. I almost wept with disappointment. I had done my best, but my opportunity was gone. Here I was, a fugitive in France, aidless and alone. My ship, the beautiful *Cicely*, was captured by the enemy, with no possibility of giving me a berth ever again. Wellstead, to whom I was apprenticed and on whom all my hopes had rested, was captured by the French, and the Mate had said that he was in a dungeon. Wars sometimes lasted thirty years or more. He was unlikely to be released. I was utterly despondent and tears began to fill my eyes.

To raise my spirits I tried to whistle 'Heart of Oak'. Whoever said that 'all ills are bearable if accompanied by food' spoke truly, and I began to feel much recovered. I got to my feet, my ankle sore but able to support me. *Come cheer up, my lads, 'tis to glory we steer.* I sang softly to myself, feeling in my pocket for another piece of cheese. *To add something more to this wonderful year.* I looked around me and saw the blue sea sparking in the sun. *To honour we call you, as freemen not slaves.* I broke off a piece of cheese and put it into my mouth, noticing ripe blackberries on a bush within reach. *For who are so free as the sons of the waves?* I pushed blackberries into my mouth, enjoying their juice, and was about to recommence my song when two French soldiers walked into the clearing.

I am sure that the lyrics of 'Heart of Oak' were not calculated to be popular among the soldiers of the French Army, but it was not out of deference to their sensibilities that I stopped singing but rather the simple fear of discovery. I dropped as quietly as I could to the ground. As I did so the piece of cheese in my hand fell into a sandy patch of earth. I gently pulled the coat over my head, leaving a crack to see out, and watched the activity in the clearing.

The day was warm, and the soldiers unbuttoned their coats, leaned their muskets against the wall of the chapel and sat down in the shade with their backs to the wall. A meal was produced from their knapsacks and they settled down to eat. Their First Consul Napoleon is subsequently supposed to have remarked that an army 'marches on its stomach', and the rations produced by the two soldiers would have made their English counterparts' mouths water with envy.

The food was placed with some care onto a cloth spread on the grass and then consumed slowly by the soldiers, who also produced a bottle of wine which they shared. I watched this ritual with great fascination, willing them to go away. Just out of reach, on the sandy soil, the great ants which abounded in the area set about making their own meal of my piece of cheese, swarming over it and carrying pieces of it off to their nests.

The soldiers did not seem to have great enthusiasm for resuming their search for the Mate, for when they had finished their meal they sat where they were, smoking several pipes of tobacco, talking in low tones which I could not hear properly above the constant drone of insects. Eventually they dozed off, their heads nodding forward onto their chests.

I was beginning to think that I should escape from the vicinity of the chapel, which seemed to be a magnet for soldiers, when a girl of about twelve came into the clearing from the path over the Cap, carrying a basket full of blackberries. She was accompanied by a small white dog, which barked noisily when it saw the soldiers sitting by the wall, running right up to them.

The soldiers jerked awake at the noise, looking up in alarm. When they saw the girl they relaxed and engaged her in conversation. She gave them some blackberries, which they ate with relish. I could not tell what they were speaking about, but I gained the impression that they knew one another and heard the phrase '*Matelot anglais*' used several times, presumably referring to the Mate.

While this conversation was going on, I watched the activities of the small white dog with growing alarm. It started to sniff round the chapel and then, finding nothing there, around the remains of the soldiers' meal, from which it was pushed away. It moved towards the edge of the clearing, walking slowly round and sniffing. With horror, I realised that it would soon reach me, and I felt for the knife in my pocket. The dog paused in its search, turned into the bushes and saw me. For a moment our eyes met and I prayed that it would keep quiet. It did not, though. It came towards me, barking. I was sure that I was discovered and started to rise to my feet.

To be saved by a piece of cheese is perhaps not heroic, but that is what happened to me. My intended repast was lying between me and the clearing, and the dog noticed it, sniffed and picked it up in its mouth. As it did so it started barking wildly, and I think that the ants on the cheese had stung it in the mouth. Still carrying the cheese and barking, it ran out of the bushes and back to its mistress, who continued talking to the soldiers. The girl looked at the dog and knelt down to pat it, speaking comforting sounding words as she did so. The dog quietened down and then ate the cheese, and the girl turned back to the soldiers, who had got to their feet and were repacking their knapsacks in an unhurried manner.

But the dog, released, ran back to my hiding place and started barking again, making what to me, a few feet away, sounded like a terrible din. I whispered, 'Good boy' and 'Go home', but the dog took no notice, by now barking quite frantically. I was sure that my capture was inevitable, and watched as first the girl and then the soldiers turned to see what was going on. Just at that moment another pair of soldiers came running into the clearing and spoke excitedly, with many animated gestures, pointing back towards the port. I guessed that the Mate's body had been found and the soldiers were required to help in the recovery effort. The original pair of soldiers hurriedly buttoned their tunics, snatched up their muskets and followed their comrades along the path.

The girl, clearly wanting to see what was going on, immediately set out after them. At the edge of the clearing she turned and shouted at the dog, which, though still barking at me, kept glancing at the retreating people. Seeing that the dog was not obeying her call, she called once more impatiently and then turned and started walking briskly along the path. Obedient to his mistress, the dog gave one final bark and was off. I lay back down on the ground, weak with fear and relief. I suppose at that stage it might have been sensible to change my hiding place, in case the dog returned, but the hour was growing late and the girl had come from over the Cap, and her basket had been full, so I reasoned that it was likely that she would return to the town when the excitement was over. Occasionally, shouts could be heard far away over the hill and I thought that the Mate's body was being recovered, probably with ropes from the top of the cliff. The shouting stopped eventually and I could hear no sound of human activity.

I rested my head on my arm and, lulled by the buzzing of insects, slept again. On reflection I think that this day of enforced idleness, largely spent lying down, was the reason for the speedy mending of my ankle. Subsequently, I have known similar injuries in people who have kept walking take weeks or even months to get better.

The sun was setting when I awoke, and the area was deserted. I ate some more food and moved to the edge of the clearing to reconnoitre. The wind had dropped, but there was still a considerable groundswell rolling in, making a heavy surf on the vast beach. The evening was very clear and I had a good vantage point. To my left was the cape and to my right the beach, perhaps half a mile wide, running in a northerly direction as far as I could see. Offshore I could see what looked like small islands quite close, dark against the setting sun, and further away, to the south-west, I could see a larger island which I thought must be Jersey. I strained my eyes and saw another island, barely visible on the horizon to the west. I thought that this must be another of the Channel Islands, and I racked my memory trying to remember Wellstead's chart. Could it be Guernsey? That the large islands were British territory was beyond doubt.

I did not know what to do. In order to get to British territory I had to cross the sea, and to do that I had to get a boat somehow. Could I go back to Carteret and steal one? I had seen boats there, but they seemed to be in the centre of the town, a town being used as a naval base. After today's events I expected that the place would be in a state of some excitement, where I was quite likely to be challenged.

Chapter 10
Spring Tide

As I watched the sun go down I started to think about what the Mate had said the previous night on the Cape. He had told me that Morlaix intended to take the *Cicely* into Weymouth and capture the King. Could this really happen? It seemed all too possible. I had several times seen the King walking along the esplanade, yards from the sea, surrounded by flunkies. True, there were naval ships at anchor in the bay, but they did not seem to be in any great state of readiness. I had no doubt that a determined group of men, for example the sailors who had boarded the *Cicely* (was it really only two days ago?), could snatch the King and take him away by boat.

The *Cicely* must be central to the whole plan. She was well known in Weymouth and her appearance there would not be remarked. She was a big ship and a considerable number of men could be concealed in her hold. The delay in her passage between London and Weymouth would not be obvious, as nobody in Weymouth would know when she had left London or where she was bound. The Mate would have been useful to the French, but I did not think that his absence would be fatal to the scheme. There must be several officers in the French Navy who spoke English well enough to be thought native, and indeed Morlaix's own accent was very slight.

The enterprise headed by Morlaix was daring in the extreme, but it could easily work. At the time, I thought of it as Morlaix's plan, but looking back I think that another, greater mind was its originator. The bold conception, the excellence of the organisation and the scale of the resources made available to it pointed to its true leader as none other than the future Emperor himself, Napoleon Bonaparte, and though I did not know it at the time, it was now Jack Stone against Napoleon.

As I sat in the clearing, watching the tide cover the wide beach with astonishing speed, a desperate plan formed in my mind, and in the gathering darkness I walked warily once more across the Cap towards the port, leaving Wellstead's coat under a bush but with the knife tucked into the sailor's rope belt beneath my clothes. As I came over the top of the hill in the dusk I could see that the *Cicely* was still alongside the wharf, her head pointing towards the sea. To my surprise, I saw that there were a large number of men working on her, despite the late hour, and I could hear the sound of sawing and hammering and occasionally voices. The ship was on the ground, but the tide was flooding strongly into the estuary. I knew by the moon that tonight would be the top of springs, the time in the cycle when the tidal range is greatest.

I settled down to watch from some undergrowth on the hill, well off the path. I could see the lights in the town further up the river, with the fishing boats still tied up. I know now that the fishing boats of that part of France stay in port during spring tides, but I wondered then why I had not seen any at sea. Gradually the workmen moved away from the ship, walking back up along the road by the estuary to the town. There were a lot of them, fifty or more I thought.

The tide continued to rise, and I saw the ship come off the ground and start to pull at her moorings. A man, a watchman I presumed, looked over the side and felt the tension in the ropes, and then went back to a small hut on the quay, which had the only lighted window closer than the town. The moon came up over the cape and illuminated the scene beneath me. A light land breeze was blowing off the shore, rippling the sea's surface, and I could see and hear the surf from the huge groundswell breaking on the beach. The rise of the tide was a fascinating phenomenon, but it seemed to me to be agonisingly slow. I saw the watchman come out of his hut again and look at the *Cicely's* ropes, but I could see that he was an old man, stooping as he walked, and I hoped that he would soon settle down in his hut for the night.

I was fairly sure that there was nobody on the ship. At about midnight the tidal stream began to slacken. I could see that the height of the tide was exceptional, as it was flooding onto the wharf near the ship and the road to the town was covered in seawater. As cautiously as I could, I moved down to the ship, my heart beating with excitement. I stopped every few yards to look round but felt confident that there was nobody except the watchman nearer to the ship than the town. I walked across the flat land near the quay as casually as I could, going from building to building and waiting while I spied out the way ahead. I had decided that to run would call attention to me if I was spotted, but if I walked I would probably be taken for a workman going back to the ship to collect something he had forgotten. The lack of a guard over the ship showed that the French had no inkling that they had any reason to be vigilant and that the death of the Mate had been taken for an accident.

As I drew near the ship, she looked huge, floating high above the wharf on the top of the tide. I was waiting in the shadow of a building which smelt like a paint store when I saw the watchman emerge and walk towards the ship to check the ropes. As he went about his rounds I inspected the ship. Piles of roundshot lay around on the quay and I knew that her cargo had at least been partially discharged. Ports had been cut in her side and I realised that cannon were being installed. Some of the ports had covers over them, so closely fitted that the openings were almost invisible. The *Cicely* was being fitted for her attack on Weymouth, and I was sure that in the hold provision was being made for the men who would be carried there.

The ship was tied up with ropes which were secured to large wooden posts driven into the wharf a considerable distance from the ship, an arrangement designed to minimise the effect of the tidal rise and fall on the ropes' tension. The posts at the bow were submerged to a depth of a foot or so and the watchman had to wade through the water to get to them, stopping at the water's edge to remove his shoes before he did so. I looked at the shoes with some envy, as I was not wearing any, according to the custom in those days of the sailor working on board ship. The temporary stand of the tide had made the ropes slack and the watchman grunted to himself as he put his hand on them. In contrast to the practice at most ports, where four ropes are used to tie up a ship, only two ropes were used here, one at the bow of the ship, and the other at the stern.

The watchman finished his inspection, put his shoes back on and went back to his hut. A curl of smoke came from a small stovepipe on its roof and I expected that he would be inside for some time. I could see that the tide was just starting to ebb towards the sea, and the ship nudged uneasily against the piles of the wharf. It was now or never. I walked as calmly as I could from the building to the post to which the ship's bowline was made fast. Though the cable was heavy, there was no tension in it at all, and it was a simple matter to lift it clear of the post and lower it into the harbour as noiselessly as I could.

I quickly moved up the wharf past the ship, on to the post holding the stern line, moving as quietly as I could through the water surrounding it. The tide was definitely ebbing now, and as I pulled on the rope, trying to get enough slack to pull it over the post, I felt the beginnings of despair. I had left it too late, there was too much tension in it. I could not possibly pull the *Cicely's* three hundred tons against the current. Throwing caution to the wind, I started to pull rhythmically on the cable, making it bounce. The noise it made slapping into the water sounded to me loud enough to wake the dead, but the watchman's hut remained quiet. Each time the cable bounced I pulled the rope a little higher up the pole, perhaps half an inch at a time. It was an agonising process, but eventually it came off the top of the post and the stern of the *Cicely* moved away in the current. I looked up to the ship and saw Wellstead's net bin on the poop deck. It seemed incredible that only yesterday I had lain hiding in that bin.

I seemed rooted to the spot, up to my knees in water, astonished and overawed by what I had done. In the course of less than twenty four hours I had killed a man and cast adrift a ship worth God knows how much.

The stern had moved perhaps twenty feet from its original position when I heard a sound from above and looked up. I had made a serious mistake. A rope had been rigged from near the top of the foremast to a post a hundred yards or so inland. The intention was clearly to ensure that the ship leaned in towards the wharf as she took the ground, and not out into the stream. This rope was now very tight, and I watched as the ship started to heel to its pull, slewing broadside to the stream, which was ebbing very quickly. It was as though someone had suddenly removed the plug from the harbour. Horrible creaking noises came from the foremast and I knew that soon something would break.

As the ship slewed, the *Cicely*'s long bowsprit swept across the wharf and jammed itself with astonishing precision through the door of a wooden store hut. Everything was horribly noisy, but no one came to investigate. I stepped forwards to try to see better what was going on, a step too far, and suddenly found myself swimming in deep swirling water, carried with bewildering speed by the tide towards the black side of the ship. My attempts to grab the wharf came to nothing and to my horror I realised that the tide was taking me to the bow of the ship, which was by now grinding into the top of the wharf with the colossal force of the *Cicely*'s weight behind it.

Then the rush of the tide submerged me and I tumbled over in the tumult of water between the ship's raked stem post and the wharf. Something caught my right ear a painful blow, but then I was through, back on the surface gasping for breath, but alive. I watched with awe as the *Cicely*'s foretopmast shrouds and the rope to the masthead broke simultaneously and the ship came suddenly upright, pirouetting slowly out into the stream.

But this was not the most astonishing sight of that night, for as the bow of the ship came in view I could see that the bowsprit had been damaged by its encounter with the building and was drooping towards the water. The bowsprit had been damaged in the fight, yes, but it had emerged the victor, for skewered on it, seemingly unable to escape, was the store hut. Though my predicament was terrible, carried headlong by the tide down the estuary towards the booming sea at the bar, I laughed at this sight. Laughed and laughed, until I was brought to my senses by swallowing seawater and began swimming as fast as I could towards the shore. It was touch and go whether I might make it or not, for the tide was running terribly fast out of the harbour, but I resisted the temptation to swim against the stream and instead, as my father had taught me, swum at right angles to it towards the land.

I was very tired when my feet touched bottom on the beach at the side of the estuary and I knew that I had made it. Looking round, I saw the *Cicely* out in the middle of the stream, heading towards the sea with her foretopmast dangling and the store hut still skewered on the bowsprit. I stayed for a moment in the shallows and then made my way across the beach to the path up the Cap. I was deadly tired but curiously elated. As I got to the top of the hill I looked back and saw her bump heavily once in the surf on the sandbar at the end of the harbour, and then again, and come to rest heavily heeled over, the tide pressing her onto the sand and the waves breaking against her. Desperate and cold as I was, I would not at that moment have swapped places with the watchman warm in his hut.

I walked along the clifftop path, stopping at the place where the path forked and the Mate had thrown his pistol at me. On an impulse I walked over to the spot where I thought the pistol had landed after I had thrown it, and by great good fortune found it almost straight away. I had no powder or shot for it, but its weight was reassuring, and I stuck it into my belt and walked on. I passed the place where I had fought the Mate, suppressing a shudder at the memory. I was very tired, and did not keep a lookout but walked with my head down. Fortunately, I did not meet anyone else on the way and before long arrived at the clearing with the ruined chapel.

I retrieved Wellstead's coat and gratefully put it on. At that moment I would have given anything for the warmth of my parents' kitchen in Portland, with my stomach full of my mother's cooking and the prospect of a sound sleep in my own warm bed. However, the coat was better than nothing, and the elation of my action in Carteret was still with me. Had anyone so young dealt such a blow to his country's enemies before? I dug around in the pockets and came up with some more food, slightly past its best, and rather mixed up together. However, it tasted wonderful and I ate until the stock was much reduced.

As I ate I wondered what was going on in the port and imagined the place by now swarming with men looking at the *Cicely* on the sandbar. There was certainly no prospect of getting her off until the tide came up again, about midday. How much damage had I done to the ship? The foremast and the bowsprit would certainly have to be replaced, but I had no idea if more serious damage had been done when she hit the bar. She was strongly built, quite new and very sound, but she had struck hard and there was a big groundswell. I was also conscious that the ship had been heeling as she was pinned to the bar by the tide and perhaps water had got in through the gunports they had cut into her side. Serve them right if it had, I thought with satisfaction. At the very least, I could be certain that I had delayed the attack on Weymouth by several days.

I imagined the recriminations beginning, and wondered if the French would think that the *Cicely*'s release from the wharf had been deliberate. The watchman would swear blind that he had checked the ropes, but would he be believed? Could they possibly imagine circumstances in which the ropes would slip from their posts accidentally? The fact that the masthead line had not been released would probably increase the likelihood of them believing that the ship had worked herself loose, for what saboteur would release only some of the ropes? With the death of the Mate only the day before, though, they might well be in the mood to discount coincidence and accident.

Chapter 11
North!

My experience of the previous day had led me to believe that if there was to be a hue and cry following the stranding of the *Cicely*, the chapel where I presently was would be a focus for searchers. I knew that I should not stay there, but could not decide where to go. In the end, I went northwards. Though Jersey was closer if I went south, England was to the north. Going south meant that I would somehow have to get round or through Carteret, an unattractive prospect. However, in front of me was the great beach, a giant deserted highway running north.

I walked down a path from the chapel to the beach and went for about half an hour along the soft sand near the dunes. I did not want to go on the harder sand near the sea, as the dunes offered some opportunity to hide if I was seen. When I felt too tired to continue I walked into the dunes, collecting some driftwood as I went. The dunes were very large, probably a hundred feet tall. Walking up them was extremely tiring, as the sand constantly gave way beneath my feet. At the top of the dunes coarse grass grew, with sharp leaves. As I walked, conies sometimes scattered in front of me, and once I saw a fox. Behind me I could see the black mass of the Cap, and I dearly wished I could see through it to the *Cicely* stranded on the sandbar. The sea was still breaking heavily and I knew that the Frenchies would not be having an easy time there.

Dawn was breaking when I found what I judged to be a suitable place to stop, a hollow near the top of a dune, with quantities of long grass growing around. As far as I could see the dunes and the beach were entirely deserted, as was the area inland, where the dunes gradually became hills and the dune grass gave way to gorse and other stunted bushes. Dropping to my knees I dug a long hole like a shallow grave in the sand, made a framework over it with pieces of driftwood and put Wellstead's coat over the top. When I had covered the coat with a layer of sand my hiding place was very inconspicuous. I crawled in, rested my head upon my arm and was instantly asleep.

I spent the next day sitting outside my hiding place in the warm sun, resting and recovering my strength. There was no sign of any activity on the beach, or on the Cap as far as I could see, and I surmised from this that the *Cicely*'s grounding was being treated either as an accident or the work of a traitor or spy in the town. The tide advanced and retreated across the beach, but the breakers had subsided noticeably since yesterday. I ate the remaining food, but it was not much and I began to feel very hungry. I was also thirsty, as there was no fresh water near my hiding place. At about three in the afternoon I could bear it no longer and decided I must go inland and find food and water. Before I set off I filled in my trench, burying Wellstead's coat as I did so, so that no trace remained of my hiding place.

I walked inland through the dunes, and gradually they became firmer underfoot until I was traversing a sandy heath, with bushes scattered about. I headed towards some birch trees and to my great joy saw that they surrounded a small pond. Sinking to my knees I drank my fill of the brown, peaty-tasting water, and then took off my clothes, which were full of salt and sand, and rinsed them. I wrung them out as well as I could and spread them on bushes in the sun. While the clothes were drying I walked round, picking blackberries and stuffing them into my mouth. I noticed that there were a great many coney droppings on the ground.

After an hour or so I put my partially dry clothes back on and, feeling much better, continued walking inland. Within about half a mile I came to the edge of a cultivated field, where the feathery leaves of carrots protruded from the sandy soil. I looked round cautiously and saw that there was a farm cottage not far distant. Watching for some time but seeing no activity, I went into the field and pulled up several bunches of carrots. They were not particularly large, but they tasted exceptionally good. I retired away from the field, carrying as many carrots as I could, and started to walk back towards the beach. As I approached the pond where I had washed my clothes, a thought struck me. There were certainly conies near the pond and they liked carrots, or so it was said. My body was crying out for food other than vegetables or fruit so I decided to try to catch one.

I took off my belt, which, in the fashion of mariners, was a piece of cord doubled up with the ends finished off with fancy splices. Using a birch sapling as a spring and a carrot as bait, I made a snare outside a burrow as I had done many times in my boyhood on Portland. I knew that English conies come out at dusk to feed and I confidently expected that French ones did the same, and when the snare was finished I went back to my hiding place among the dunes, carrying some dry furze back with me.

My camp place was undisturbed and there was still no sign of activity on the beach, so I dug a hole in the valley between two dunes and took out the Mate's pistol. After many attempts I managed to coax enough spark out of it to start the furze smouldering and, by dint of careful blowing, eventually to burst into flame. I think that the sight of a fire is always cheering and comforting, and my pleasure and satisfaction was greatly increased because of the difficulty I had had in making it.

I lay down again and dozed until the sun set and then went back to the pond to see if I had caught anything. I had – a nice fat buck which I immediately took back to the beach and prepared with the knife, not too fussily for I was hungry for the meat. Using the technique I had practised that afternoon, I lit a small fire with the pistol and soon had the meat and some carrots cooking. I was concerned that the fire might be seen or smelt, so I kept well away from it, going back occasionally to turn the meat or put more fuel on the fire. Cooking took an hour or so. As soon as it was finished I extinguished the fire, burying the embers, and took the food to a nearby dune. While I have no doubt that the meal if served in the galley of a merchant ship would have led to dissatisfaction on the part of the diner, it definitely fitted the bill as far as I was concerned, and I ate with relish.

When the meal was finished I felt much better, but realised that unless I moved straight away I would go to sleep where I was until morning. I resolved to go immediately and put the remaining food into the coat pockets with the knife and pistol. In the moonlight, thus equipped, I left the cover of the dunes and walked along the beach – to the north, in the direction of England – following the strand line. The sand was quite hard and the going was easy, akin to walking on a road. I had been going for three hours or so when the beach narrowed round a low rocky headland. As the tide was low I was able to walk round this obstacle, but I knew that at high tide the sea would come right up to the rocks.

I continued along the beach, eventually noticing that the sky was paling towards the east. I knew I should find a hiding place, but the feeling that I was at last travelling in the right direction for home was so intoxicating that the idea of stopping was unbearable. As the light increased I saw that the beach narrowed and came to an end a couple of miles or so ahead and that a high headland, well wooded, jutted out into the sea there. I decided that, light or no light, I would walk until I reached that headland, and then find a place to hide.

The sun was up by the time I reached the cape and it felt terribly exposed walking along the beach, but I saw nobody at all. There was no obvious path up the headland so I started to climb through the trees, greatly impeded by undergrowth. The trees were small but tangled closely together. On reaching the top of the hill the wood ended abruptly and fields began. Quite close by stood a farmhouse, built of grey stone, with some outlying buildings round a small yard. I saw chickens scrambling round a woman with a basket scattering food for them. The woman was the first person I had seen since the watchman in Carteret.

In the distance, perhaps half a mile away, I could see a small village clustered round a church with a square tower. It would be dangerous for me to try to cross the fields in daylight and so I walked through the woods towards the sea. Nearing the cliff the woods became thinner and were eventually replaced by gorse and long grass. With great caution I walked across this relatively open ground until I stood on the top of the cliff, which was several hundred feet high. The great beach stretched out to the south as far as the eye could see, but my view to the north was obstructed as I was not at the highest point of the headland. The sea was calm and blue. Far away I could see a smudge on the horizon, one of the Channel Islands. As I watched, several fishing boats appeared around the northern end of the headland, driven by lug sails. The boats were crewed by a single fisherman and my heart leaped when I saw them, as I realised that there was a fishing harbour just to the north of the headland.

I walked back into the woods, very tired by now, sat down and ate the remains of my food. Several times as I ate my head nodded forward, and I awoke each time with a start. I was so tired that when I lay down, wrapped in the coat, the ground felt as soft as a down bed and I immediately fell into a deep dreamless sleep.

The day was well advanced when the sound of children's voices woke me. Though I could not see them, I could hear their progress across the fields to the clifftop, where they stayed for some time, and then back the way they had come, presumably either to the cottage or the village. After my recent experience I was glad that they were not accompanied by a dog, but the incident made me realise how vulnerable my position was, and I knew that my capture was inevitable if I stayed in France. I must get away.

As the evening advanced the fishing boats returned, going close inshore round the north side of the headland, to the unseen port which I knew must be there. As so often happens on Channel coasts in summer, the wind dropped with the sun. In the calm, the last boats to arrive were propelled round the headland by a single oar used as a scull over the stern. I was once again becoming hungry and thirsty. Remembering the chickens I had seen that morning in the farmyard, I decided to steal one if possible. I walked through the wood to the part nearest to the cottage, and then across the fields to within fifty yards or so of it, picking carrots as I went.

I settled down by a hedge to see where the occupants of the cottage might be. There was no activity outside, but light came from some of the windows and it seemed that the family had retired for the night. I realised that the chickens must be inside one of the buildings round the yard, or in a coop. Satisfied that I would not be observed, I slowly made my way towards the house. Near it I made out what I thought was the hen house against a wall on the other side of the yard. In the yard was a water trough. I was making my way to it, round the yard with my back pressed to the wall of an outbuilding, when to my horror I heard footsteps approaching. I pressed myself against the wall of the building, and then, with more haste than silence, dived in through its open doorway.

The building was little more than three walls and a roof and seemed to be used as a store for tools and wood, indistinct in the near darkness. I concealed myself as well as I could behind a small cart and watched as the gate at the far side of the yard opened, and a tall man dressed in a smock and cap entered, carrying two pails, one large and one small. I expected that he would turn left through the gate and go to the house, but he did not and instead walked purposefully across the yard straight to the building where I was inadequately concealed. As he approached there seemed something familiar about him, perhaps his gait or dress, and I realised with a start that he was a fisherman.

This was confirmed as he entered the building, quite close to me, and I smelled the odour of fishing boat and of my boyhood. Anyone who has ever owned, or gone to sea in a fishing boat will know the smell, composed of elements of tar, fish, bilge water and mud, and quite unmistakable. He put the larger of the two pails down on a bench in the store, and I wondered what was in it. Without suspecting my presence, he walked back to the house and I saw him against the light from inside as he made his way in. Before the door closed I heard the excited voices of children and the calmer voice of a woman welcoming home the man of the house.

These sounds were very affecting to me, as they reminded me so much of my childhood, welcoming home my father on his return from sea. It was becoming darker, and as I waited in the outbuilding I could see in through the lighted window of the house as the family sat down to eat their meal. The man had taken off his smock and sat at the table with the children, a boy and girl, while the woman put bowls of food in front of them. I watched as the woman took her place opposite her husband and the family bowed their heads as grace was said. This was almost more than I could bear. It seemed so unfair that though I was separated from these people and their familiar life by no more than a few feet, I was forced to inhabit a different world, of danger and uncertainty. I had only wanted to be an apprentice on the *Cicely*, nothing more. What had happened to me? Who had decided that I should be the enemy of these people? Was it the King? I did not know, but at that moment the idea of fighting the French, so like us, seemed a dreadful thing.

My eyes streamed with tears and I think I was very close to knocking on the door and giving myself up; it was only the memory of the Mate's words 'French dungeon' that kept me from so doing. I eventually recovered and moved stealthily to inspect the pail that the man had brought with him. I hoped that it might contain fish which I could steal, but to my disappointment there was only a long thin line inside, studded with hooks. I could see through the window that the family was busy with their meal, talking and laughing. I surmised that the day's fishing had been good and thought that a man who had a farm with a good house, a wife and healthy children, and a fishing boat nearby was someone who wanted for nothing in life.

Leaving the outbuilding, I crept across the yard to the water trough. When I had drunk all I could and washed my face, I went over to the chicken coop. The chickens were quiet inside the coop, which was a wooden structure about eight by four feet, with a wooden lattice door. I was not an expert on catching or killing chickens so had to stop and think carefully about what to do. When my plan was decided I opened the door as slowly and quietly as I could and reached inside for the nearest chicken, which to my amazement took no notice of me. As my hand approached, the chicken began to move slightly and let out a low cluck. Suddenly, I grabbed it by the neck, squeezing as hard as I could. The chickens erupted in noise, cackling and beating their wings. I dragged the chicken with its wings flapping out of the coop, shut the door quickly and noisily with my left hand, and ran out of the yard towards the field as fast as I could, the struggling chicken held tight to my chest. The chicken was big and strong, but I was determined not to let it go.

I had gone only a few yards into the field, running fast, when I tripped and fell heavily onto my face, knocking the wind completely out of me but seemingly doing more damage to the chicken, which ceased to struggle. Gasping for breath, I looked back towards the house and saw the door open and the man put his head out, looking towards the hen house. Apparently satisfied with what he saw, he went back in and shut the door. I lay still on my chicken mattress for some time, thankful that the fisherman had not turned his head in my direction, for I was easily visible from the house.

As soon as I could I got up and walked towards the woods, swinging the chicken as I went.

***

My walk back was difficult in the darkness, with branches and brambles tearing at me. Eventually I found the place where I had slept and set about preparing the chicken. I had never realised that a chicken had so many feathers, and as I pulled them from the bird set about burying them in a small pit I had dug in the earth, so they would not scatter and lead searchers to my hiding place. With the same technique as the day before, I made a small fire, hidden as much as possible in a pit. I had cut the chicken into small pieces, but it was quite a long time before they were all cooked. The chicken tasted delicious though rather black on the outside and a bit raw on the inside, and I ate it with more carrots taken from the field near the farm.

After that, I stowed away my stores and accoutrements in Wellstead's coat, which was by now looking rather sorry for itself, and set out to follow the clifftop. The moon rose, shining on the sea. After a few hundred yards I reached the point of the cape and shortly afterwards could see the view towards the north. In the distance was a surf- lined beach and, nestling in the shelter of the cape, a small harbour, rather exposed looking with houses set back from its edge. I knew that this must be the destination of the fishing boats I had seen earlier, and on looking closely I could see there were several alongside the mole which gave the harbour some protection. To me the boats represented escape and salvation, and I knew that I must steal one.

The face of the cape nearest the harbour was a rocky cliff, not quite vertical, but much too steep to climb down in the near darkness. There had to be a road from the village to the port, as the chicken's former owner had clearly walked up from his boat. I therefore struck inland, at first through grass and gorse and then across fields. Eventually I saw the church tower against the sky, quite close, and then there was a hedge, and the road visible behind it, white in the moonlight. I walked along the hedge until I came to a gate, and after waiting for some time to ensure there was nobody about, climbed over it onto the road.

The walk down the road was nerve racking in the extreme, for if I met anybody on that narrow way I would have no escape. I stopped every hundred yards or so and listened. The road led in a winding way down the cape and I had not been walking for very long before I saw the harbour in front of me; it would be an exposed place in an easterly wind, like Swanage, the Dorset town not far from my home in Portland. The tide was high and the fishing boats were floating, but I expected that this harbour, like Carteret to the south, would dry out at low tide. A road separated the houses from the harbour and there were no houses close to the mole. The town was not large and to me looked rather poor.

I decided to walk towards the mole to obtain a better idea of the layout of the port and a closer look at the fishing boats. After some minutes I stopped amongst some large rocks at the start of the mole and examined the boats made fast to it. They were not large, between twenty and twenty-five feet long, and beamy. They seemed sturdy and heavy, and were decked for about half their length, with a pronounced sheerline. All had a single mast setting a lug sail, with a large oar hanging over the stern. Wooden legs were fitted to their sides to stop them falling over when they took the ground.

I thought about the tides. I guessed that the time was then about two o'clock in the morning and the tide was high. Low tide the previous evening had been about seven. The fisherman had appeared at the house about ten, which meant that there was enough water in the harbour for his boat two or three hours each side of low water. Before I could successfully escape in a stolen boat, several factors had to be considered. There had to be enough water to float the boat, enough wind to sail it, I had to have some idea of the local geography, and to escape swift capture I had to be out of sight of the nearby cape by dawn.

I was becoming very uneasy at my close proximity to the town, though no lights were showing, and decided that I had seen all that I needed. I retraced my steps back along the road up the cape, walking even more cautiously than on the way down. By now the moon had disappeared and it was quite dark, and it was with considerable relief that I found myself back at my hiding place in the woods. Before falling asleep, questions popped into my mind. Did farmers' wives know how many chickens they had? Did they count them very often? Would a stolen chicken precipitate a search for the thief? Would I ever sleep with a roof over my head again?

I think I was becoming nocturnal for I did not wake the next day until late afternoon. I ate cold chicken and carrots and found some blackberries to slake my thirst. With great caution, for I could not bear the prospect of being caught after all my tribulations, I moved over the cape to a spot in the long grass overlooking the harbour. It was probably about four o'clock in the afternoon when I looked over the cliff. The tide was quite high and I could see the fishing boats tied up alongside the mole, with people working on them and nearby. While I had slept they had been to sea and their day's work was now over.

As I waited on the headland for darkness to fall, the weather, which for the past few days had been fair, began to change. The sky became cloudy and light rain started to fall. The wind, which until then had been a light sea breeze blowing onto the land, began to blow from the south-west, fitfully at first, but then more steadily, driving the rain unpleasantly.

When it was dark I ate more chicken and carrots, and walked back across the fields to the road. As before it was deserted, but I was still wary, and on reaching the mole I waited in the shelter of the rocks as before, wanting to be sure that there were no fishermen mending their nets or working on their boats. I looked back towards the town. No lights could be seen in the windows and I thought that the fishermen would be asleep early, as the tide dictated an early start in the morning. The harbour was dry and the fishing boats were on the ground, but I knew that the tide was on the rise and would soon come flooding in. The weather had not improved and there was a light driving rain. This was the moment!

With my heart beating in my chest, I left the shelter of the rocks and walked along the mole, looking at the boats. They were all similar, and I chose one that seemed to be well kept, tied up at the end of the mole nearest the sea. I could just make out the name *Jean René* on her bows in large letters as I found a rope and slid down it onto the boat. She was about twenty feet long and there was a small cuddy or shelter under the foredeck, just forward of the single mast. The boat's gear looked in good condition and it was laid out in a way that was very similar to my father's boat. I was sure that I would be able to sail her, but before I would have the opportunity to prove this, there had to be enough water for her to float. The rising tide had wetted her keel by now and I knew that it would not be long before she would be lifted off the ground completely.

By this time the wind had increased, still from the southwest, driving penetrating drizzle before it. I realised that the visibility would not be good when I got out to sea, but I was determined to go. I had been a mariner all my life and it was wonderful for me to be back on a boat, especially a fishing boat like my father's. I had intended to get off the boat after my inspection and wait for the tide ashore, but I felt so at home that I decided to hide in the cuddy in the bows. I opened the low door and got into the cramped space amidst coils of rope, nets and buoys.

As I lay in my dark hiding place, I heard the water lapping up the side of the boat, until, after what seemed an age, the boat moved uneasily in the harbour waves and started to bump against the bottom and quay. I knew that I must resist the temptation to try to leave the harbour too early, as my escape attempt would come to an ignominious end if the boat ended up aground in the entrance to the harbour. I waited in an agony of impatience for the tide to rise further, until I could bear it no longer and opened the door. The strength of the wind came as some surprise, but the drizzle had stopped. When I looked along the mole towards the shore, though, my heart sank. Approaching the fishing boats, not more than a hundred yards away, was someone carrying a lantern. What could I do? There was no hiding place on the mole, and there was no possibility of me getting past the person on the mole without being seen. My only option was to stay on the boat and hope that the person approaching was not *Jean René's* owner, come to check the bilges or mooring ropes. As quietly as I could I got back inside the cuddy, closing the door until there was just a crack for me to see out of. For a while nothing was visible, and then, suddenly, the lantern came into view, startlingly close. To my astonishment the person carrying the lamp was the woman I had seen in the house the night before. It seems foolish now but I immediately assumed that she knew me to be the chicken rustler and had tracked me down to exact vengeance.

As she came close enough for me to see her face, illuminated by the lantern, I realised it was not the loss of the chicken that was worrying her. She wore an expression which I had seen many times on my own mother's face when my father had not returned from the sea at the time expected, and I knew that it was concern for her husband that had brought her down to the mole.

She walked with purpose, and I think she intended to go to the end of the mole and show the lantern there, to guide her husband into the harbour. As she came parallel with the *Jean René*, however, I saw her face break out into a smile and she shouted loudly, waving the lantern vigorously. I knew that she had seen her husband returning, and though I could not see the returning boat from the cuddy, I heard a sail shaking and then a rope landed on the mole, which the woman caught expertly and made fast to an iron ring.

For the next quarter of an hour or so I listened to the sounds of the boat being tied up and the catch unloaded. Eventually I watched from the crack in the door as the fisherman and his wife walked up the mole, carrying heavy pails.

Chapter 12
The Race of Alderney

By now *Jean René* had several feet of water under her keel, and I knew that I must leave immediately or I might be seen by the fishermen who would start work at first light. The wind was quite strong by now and I remembered the old rhyme

A Devon man reefs in harbour,
A Cornishman not he!
But he who reefs never at all,
With the fishes soon shall be.

Though from Dorset, I was with the men of Devon on this question, and I decided that I would reef the sail while I was alongside. It took me a long time in the darkness with the unfamiliar sail, but at last it was finished. I tried some experimental strokes with the huge sculling oar and then, weak with excitement, cast off the mooring ropes.

I may have been free of France, but my troubles were by no means over. With the sculling oar I got the boat off the mole and moving slowly out to sea. As I left the mole I realised that the wind was stronger than I had expected. The boat began to move with the pressure of the wind on the bare mast, and I stowed the sculling oar and went to the tiller. The sea was still relatively flat and I decided that I should get sail on her. I rounded up into the wind as far as she would go and moved forward to the mast. It took me a little time to sort out the ropes, but slowly I got the sail up. It flogged severely in the strong wind and shook the whole boat. When all was secure, I moved quickly to the tiller, sheeted in the sail and we were off! The wake hissed alongside as the boat heeled over and tore through the night, the tiller vibrating in my hands.

The land would not be visible for much longer and, with the overcast sky obscuring the stars, my only guide would be the direction of the wind. As long as the wind stayed south-west and I kept the boat as close as I could to the wind, I would be sailing roughly west, towards the Channel Island I had seen the day before. In my exhilaration at the boat's progress, I did some sums in my head. The island was about twenty-five miles away. With the boat running at five knots I should be there in five hours!

My exhilaration was short lived. The boat came out from the shelter of the cape and the wind increased, laying her over. The waves suddenly became larger and more confused, and the motion of the boat quite violent. I knew from the feel of the waves that we were in a tide race, where the waves are disturbed by an uneven seabed and by the wind blowing against the tide. Suddenly there was a loud hissing sound and a breaking crest hit the boat a violent blow, laying her over so far that water poured in over the gunwale. I let the sheet go completely and the boat came upright, but there was a lot of water in her, sloshing knee deep over the bottom boards, and she floated low and sluggishly, with more water slopping into her. I ran forward to the mast, let the halyards go, and the sail fell in confusion. I left it where it was and groped in the cuddy for the bailing bucket I knew was there.

There is no activity more exhausting than bailing out a flooded boat at sea. The work is heavy and continuous, and if the boat is of any size, progress is so slow that it is almost imperceptible. The bailer cannot rest, for if he does the water level will rise. His energy is sapped by the motion of the boat and its attendant small injuries, and by fear and cold. He is motivated by self-preservation and therefore drives himself to the limit of his strength. I worked to a monotonous rhythm, 'one and two and three and one and two and three,' in a daze of fatigue, but I gradually gained on the water coming in, making the boat more buoyant. As she floated higher she shipped less solid water, though spray still came aboard. After an hour or so I was down to the level of the bottom boards, and I stopped bailing and sat trembling with exhaustion on the seat near the wildly swinging tiller.

My fear of drowning had abated, to be replaced by the familiar fear of discovery. I had to get away from the coast. I got up from the seat and roughly furled the sail, which was now dragging overboard, making it fast with a piece of rope. The boat was laying with the wind on the port bow, drifting astern. Eventually, after much trying, I got her round so that the wind was on the port quarter and she started to move through the water at two or three knots, shipping occasional crests which kept me wet through and busy with the bailing bucket.

I sailed on for an hour or so, until I realised that, though the wind was blowing as strongly as ever, the sea was much calmer and this was probably because the tide had turned. Waves in the open sea are generally regular, but if a strong tide is running in the opposite direction to the wind, the result is a wave pattern that is irregular and confused. This 'wind against tide' phenomenon can be seen along many parts of the coast where the tide runs strongly, such as in the Solent. I had just observed the state of the sea change dramatically when the tide turned, and this meant that the tide was strong and was now running north.

I knew what I should do. To hell with the Channel Islands, I would sail straight for England. 'Never waste a fair wind,' that was Wellstead's motto, and I was sure that the same logic applied to tides. The Channel Islands were a long way off the coast, probably encumbered by off-lying rocks, and the visibility was so poor that I could sail straight past them. England, though further away, was a big place and I could hardly fail to hit it. The wind was fair for England and so was the tide, and that was where I should go.

I gybed the boat round so that the wind was on the starboard quarter and ran to the north, or what I hoped was north. The boat was much quieter now and I decided to set some sail. As soon as I did, the boat tramped ahead with a great foaming wave at her forefoot. She was over canvassed, without doubt, and broached occasionally, but I did not care. I was going home.

It was the wildest sail I have ever had in my life. As a grey dawn broke, revealing the size of the waves, on the starboard beam I could just about make out the French coast, probably distant about three miles, but I could see no sign of the Channel Islands. I ran northwards, keeping the coast in sight, though it was frequently obscured by rain showers. The land slid by at an amazing rate. The sun rose, giving some welcome warmth, for I was beginning to get very cold. I munched on the last pieces of chicken.

Though cold, tired and hungry, I was feeling very pleased with myself and edged in towards the coast, so as not to lose it if the showers became persistent rain. I was doing very well, I thought, and at this rate would soon be in England. I began to wonder what part of England I would hit and whether I would make it before darkness set in, when I was startled back to reality by a loud shout. I turned my head, and there, not fifty yards behind me, was a ketch of fifty tons or so with a tricouleur flying at her peak – a *chasse-marée*. She hailed me again, but still I held my course. She was now abeam and any hopes I had that she was just giving a friendly greeting were dashed when she matched my speed by reducing canvas. Another hail and I waved my hand and tried to shout something French sounding, but my voice came out as a low croak which I am sure they did not hear.

The ketch surged close to me and I saw a sailor on her with a heaving line at the ready. She hailed me again and I realised with despair in my heart that they intended to take me in tow. To this day I do not fully understand why they wanted to do this, but I expect that they were suspicious of a fishing boat so far offshore in bad weather, steering a purposeful course and unable to answer simple questions.

The *chasse marée* was very close now, plunging heavily in

the large waves, the name *Bernadette* visible on her counter. The sailor on the deck threw the heaving line, which fell across the foredeck of my boat. I rushed up and pretended to try to retrieve it, but instead managed to push it back overboard. I could see a rain shower approaching and decided on a desperate move.

The sailor pulled the heaving line in and threw it again, but it missed by some margin. The shower had now arrived and it was raining heavily. It was now or never. The seaman threw the line for the third time and it landed across *Jean René*'s cockpit. I picked it up and threw it back into the sea. Simultaneously, I put the helm down and, luffing up, headed east towards the coast. It took some time for the ketch to react, but before I lost sight of her in the rain I saw that she was turning to intercept me. I immediately tacked round and out to sea, the boat sailing fast with the wind on the beam, stinging showers of spray driving over her, heeling heavily with the lee gunwale on the waterline.

The shower cleared after a few minutes and I saw the ketch about a mile astern, heading towards the coast. She saw me and tacked, crowding on sail. *Jean René* was going as she probably had never done in her life before, plunging over the waves and flinging up spray from the weather bow, but when I looked back I knew there would be no escape. The *chasse-marée*'s skipper was driving her hard and she was sailing fast, heeled over till her lee rail was awash. She was throwing up great clouds of spray, and occasionally she dipped her long bowsprit, shipping waves green which foamed along the deck and swirled away in the scuppers. She was probably going twice as fast as me in my twenty footer.

In minutes she was a cable's length away, crossing *Jean René*'s stern to get to weather. It had started to rain again, but I did not think that I would be able to pull the same trick twice, for I could see the men on deck, crouching behind the deckhouse, ready to work the ship as soon as orders were given. She was very close now and I could see a man on her deck preparing to speak through a trumpet and, more ominously, sailors were gathered round a gun on her poop deck. There was nothing I could do. I knew that at such range, even in the wild sea that was running, it would at most take only a few rounds of grapeshot for the gunners on the ketch to find their mark. With bitter disappointment in my heart I decided that capture was better than death, and I stood up with the tiller wedged against my legs, raising my hands in what I hoped was a gesture of surrender.

I looked anxiously to the ketch to judge the reaction of her crew to my signal, but to my astonishment I saw that the man with the speaking trumpet and the crew of the swivel had lost interest in me and were looking to the west. As I watched, the *chasse marée's* helmsman spun the wheel, the men behind the deckhouse sprang into action and the ketch bore up and headed off close hauled towards the south, her hull almost enveloped in driving spray.

I felt my knees weaken and sat back down at the tiller, wondering at this turn of events. Suddenly, out of the rain a few cables length distant came a warship flying a huge British ensign. She was sailing fast, well heeled over, and I recognised her as the *Waterwitch* which had intercepted the *Cicely* on her way to Carteret. The relief I felt after all this time as a fugitive was immense. After all my struggles rescue was at hand. I was saved!

As I got to my feet to wave I saw a puff of smoke appear on the frigate, heard a bang and saw the splash as a shot fell into the sea about a hundred yards from me. Another shot rang out, but I did not see it fall, and then the frigate had passed me, sailing fast in the direction that the *Bernadette* had gone. This was a low point of my adventure. To have come so far just to have the Royal Navy shoot at me when I badly needed their aid was too much for me to bear. I sat back down at the tiller and laid my head on it, completely overcome by the emotions I had experienced in the last hour or so. Elation, despair and relief were combined now with indignation. For the second time in five days I watched the *Waterwitch*, whose aid I desperately needed, show me her stern, as she set off in the pursuit of prize money.

I was all in, physically and emotionally – cold and tired beyond endurance, I could do no more. Eventually I recovered enough to go forward and lower the sail, for by now the tide had turned again and the waves were rough and confused. I knew that I had to get out of the wind for a while, so I crawled into the cuddy and, wet though I was, fell asleep. I do not know how long I slept, but when I awoke I could tell by the motion of the boat that the weather was quieter.

I looked round in the dim light and saw that a rough set of tarpaulin garments were swinging from a nail at the side of the doorway – smock, trousers and hat. Pushing open the door with my foot, as light flooded in I saw to my great joy that there was a large sausage hanging on the other side of the door, swinging like a pendulum as the boat rolled. Further inspection resulted in discovery of a jug of cider and some hard biscuits in a tub. I sat in the cuddy eating and drinking, and as I ate my determination rose. If the Royal Navy wouldn't help me, I would have to help myself. The coast of England could only be sixty or so miles away. In my life I had sailed thousands of miles – I could do it.

I took off Wellstead's coat and put on the tarpaulins, which fitted me fairly well. The wind had dropped to a moderate breeze and there was a soft drizzle, which reduced visibility to a few hundred yards. There was no sign of any land and I could see no ships. I raised the sail but soon realised that it was too reefed, so I shook out the reefs, and soon *Jean René* was bowling along with the breeze on her port quarter. I could not see the sun, but the horizon seemed brighter in the direction from which the breeze was coming and this confirmed my view that the wind was still south-west.

The change in the weather, combined with my sleep, the food and my windproof clothes made me feel much better, and I sang as I sailed. Although the sea was by now almost flat, I had for some time been aware of tide rips and swirls in the sea, similar but on a much larger scale to those I had seen in Hurst Narrows. Though I did not know it at the time, I was in the stretch of water known as the Race of Alderney, where the tides are as fierce as anywhere in the world and in some places run at up to nine knots, producing violent overfalls.

I knew that I must be going with the tide through some narrow passage, and was keeping a good lookout when I saw an evil-looking group of rocks ahead, about twenty feet high and with the swell breaking white on them. The tide was running with breathtaking rapidity, carrying me towards them, and I could see the waves that the current made as it swept past the rocks, for all the world like the bow wave of a fast-moving ship.

I put the helm up and *Jean René* gybed as I headed her bow away from the rocks. For a few minutes I was in an agony of suspense as the boat was swept by that incredible force to within yards of the reef, so close that I could hear the noise of the tide like a cataract in a river, but much greater, and over the side I could see submerged fangs of rocks rushing past in the clear water, fronds of kelp waving in the tide.

And then we were past, completely unscathed. Shaking, I put the boat again on what I hoped was a northerly course, and for the next hour or so I believe my lookout was as good as any that has ever been kept in the history of seafaring.

***

It was becoming quite dark as the tide rips and swirls abated, and I hoped that I was now in the open Channel, the Channel of England, clear of the French coast. I had some more food, and was heartened when the sky cleared and the stars briefly appeared. I found the pole star and realised that my course was indeed pretty much northerly.

I experimented with lashing the helm and eventually got *Jean René* to sail herself more or less on course, allowing me to lie on the bottom boards and doze, covered by Wellstead's coat, waking every few minutes to bring her back on course and adjust the lashing.

In this way I spent the night. My periods asleep on the bottom boards grew longer as the night progressed, and when I awoke after one particularly lengthy horizontal period the dawn was breaking. The visibility seemed to be quite good, but though I looked eagerly ahead for land, I could see nothing.

Jean René was behaving well and I felt a surge of affection for the boat, though this was mingled with sadness as I reflected that I had deprived some poor fisherman of the benefit of her ownership, for I knew only too well how the loss of a boat could bring hardship to a fishing family. I hoped that the fishermen of *Jean René's* home port were as willing as those of Portland to help a fellow mariner in time of distress.

Weary beyond measure, I decided that as nothing was in view and the boat was sailing well I would have one more session on the cockpit sole. When I awoke some time later, feeling much better, I was greeted by one of the most ominous-looking sunrises I had ever seen.

> *Red sky at night*
> *Sailorman's delight.*
> *Red sky in the morning*
> *Sailorman's warning.*

This weather lore in my experience is seldom wrong, and the sky to the east was a blaze of red, interspaced with threatening black clouds. I calculated quickly. It was about sixty miles from Weymouth to France. I had left the vicinity of France at about ten the previous night so should now have about forty miles to go. If the wind held and I concentrated on getting the best out of *Jean René*, I might be there in ten hours. Let it blow, I thought, as I ate the last of the sausage and drank some cider, I haven't come this far to be stopped by a capful of wind.

Yet my present predicament was one of a lack of wind,

as the boat was for several hours either stopped or moving very slowly, with the sea a glassy calm, sometimes relieved by catspaws rippling the surface. Large jellyfish pulsed in the water alongside, but other than these I saw nothing at all, no ships and no land. I tried sculling with the huge oar, but progress was very slow in comparison with the energy expended and I soon gave it up. The sun was quite warm when it came out from the clouds, and my clothes dried out, though they were stiff and uncomfortable with salt and chafed my body.

It was late in the afternoon when the wind came, from the south-west. Before long *Jean René* was bowling along before it, a fine bone in her teeth. The sea came up surprisingly quickly and I decided that it was time to pull down a reef. As so often happens, it was only when I pointed the boat up into the wind to reduce sail that I realised its full strength. The wind continued to increase as it grew dark. I put the ship's head up into the wind, lowered the sail, reefed it, and was just about to hoist it when I got my right hand in between the gaff and the mast. As the boat rolled, the sail bellowed and snapped, and my hand was crushed most painfully. I stood back from the mast, holding my hand, and slowly lost consciousness, watching as the bottom boards seemed to drift up to meet me, and noting with detached interest the loud crunch as they hit my forehead.

I was roused by water in my nose, and as I raised my head I realised immediately that the boat had shipped a considerable quantity of water. Nursing my hand I got the bailing bucket out of the cuddy and bailed in a haze of pain until the water was down to the bottom boards. The wind was shrieking round the boat as I one-handedly lashed the sail. I could not see exactly what was wrong with my hand, but it was extremely painful still and there was blood on it. Perhaps I had broken one or more fingers. I sat at the helm and managed to get the boat before the wind.

Even with the sail furled, *Jean René* drove headlong

through the night, the wind now a full gale. I clung grimly to the tiller with my good hand, weak with pain. I could see nothing except the occasional foaming crest, looming white and noisy out of the darkness. All I could do was to keep the boat before the wind. Occasionally I dropped into sleep, sometimes to be brought suddenly awake by my head hitting the tiller, sometimes by the boat straying off course, the gale blowing spray and rain straight into my face, and sometimes by the shock of a breaking crest coming into the boat. Several times during that terrible night I was forced to bail the boat, a slow and painful process with my injured hand.

As I sat with the tiller pressed into my chest, cold and numb, my mind wandered so that I did not know whether I was awake or dreaming. I imagined that I was already ashore, walking across a sunny meadow, or that I was in my parent's house in Portland. Once, I seemed to have a long conversation with Wellstead, and several times I had visions of the horrible fight with the Mate.

The gale seemed to have been blowing for ever when I was woken by some perception of change in the sea. I looked round but could see nothing. The wind still blew with incredible ferocity, and the boat tore along wildly. Suddenly, as *Jean René* rose on a wave, I saw that sight most terrible to the mariner, a line of white ahead in the darkness. It was gone as quickly as it had appeared, but I knew that it was no illusion. A few seconds later I saw it again, closer now. With a sick feeling I brought the boat round to port, standing up at the helm and looking round as the boat heeled wildly. Looming out of the darkness was a wave, huge and black, surmounted by a white crest which toppled down its front as I watched. I brought the boat so that she was exactly stern on to the wave, and gripped the tiller as hard as I could, for I knew that I could do no more. There was a great roaring noise and the boat was picked up as by an invisible hand, stern skywards, and hurled forwards with incredible speed. The horrible sensation seemed to last forever, but it was brought to an abrupt end as the bow dug into the trough of the wave and the boat pitchpoled end over end, the stern cartwheeling high in the air, tearing the tiller out of my one good hand and sending me tumbling out of the cockpit.

Suddenly I was swimming, the water surprisingly warm. I could not see *Jean René* and supposed that she had sunk. I dimly realised that there was a dark line against the sky and that this could be nothing other than a cliff, quite close. I struck out for the shore, but my swimming was greatly hampered by my tarpaulin clothes, which I could not remove with my injured hand. There was another roar and a breaker flung me forward. From then on as I struggled feebly towards land I was picked up by a succession of breakers. Some just dumped me, tumbling over beneath the surface, but some rushed me forwards towards the cliff.

I had been in the water for some time when I realised that I could go on no longer. I was so exhausted that I could not move my limbs. I had swallowed large quantities of sea water, and some had gone into my lungs, making me rasp for breath. I knew that the next breaker would finish me, and I waited for its arrival, unable to struggle, floating on my back. When the wave came it was not large, and it picked me up without submerging me, just washing over my face. The wave had turned me onto my side, and as I twisted round my injured hand touched something, sending waves of pain up my arm. I floated there for some time, waiting for the next wave, when it slowly dawned on me that my hand had come into contact with the shore and the water was very shallow. I tried to stand up, but my legs were so weak that I could not, and I pulled my way ashore with my one good hand clawing for grip on the smooth flat rocks, my body floating until the water was shallow enough for me to crawl.

At length I reached dry land. England!

Chapter 13
Brandy Bay

I felt the sand in my hand, coarse and with little round pebbles in it. I remembered the smooth flat rocks I had crawled over and knew at once that I was on familiar ground – Brandy Bay.

Brandy Bay, about half way along the coast between Weymouth and Poole, is a forbidding place, with high dark cliffs made of shale which the local people burnt. I would not like to say exactly how it had become familiar to me, but it was a lonely place, well away from prying eyes.

By the time dawn broke I was strong enough to get to my feet and walk slowly along the foreshore. I knew that the cliffs here were too high and steep for me to climb, but that there was a small settlement at Kimmeridge Bay to the east. The foreshore was difficult going. At first there was dark sand with isolated rocks, but before long the sand gave way to a jumble of flat rocks, often separated by several feet. I had to jump between these rocks, which were sometimes slippery with seaweed. Eventually I came to a low point of land with a waterfall falling down it. I could not climb up the point, as the black rock was slippery and vertical and the sea was washing round it, with waves occasionally breaking quite hard against it.

The south-west wind had been replaced by a north-westerly, and the sky had cleared with puffy clouds, tinged with pink in the east. Across the furious maelstrom of breakers in Kimmeridge Bay I could see houses and boats drawn up on the slipway, and I knew that inside those houses would be people, English people who would help me. Behind me, in the distance, I could see the bulk of Portland – home.

I stood looking at the obstacle. I had lost track of the time and state of the tides and did not know what would happen if I waited. Either the tide would drop and I would be able to walk round dry shod, or it would rise and I would be cut off and perhaps have nowhere to go if the beach completely disappeared at high water. Gathering my remaining strength, I waited for a promising-looking pause in the waves and set out as fast as I could to the safety of the rocks on the other side of the waterfall. The waterfall soaked me, my feet slipped on the green slime growing beneath it, and I sat hard and painfully on the rocks, struggling to get to my feet as a wave approached, hissing from the sea. It was not much of a wave, but it picked me up and dragged me for a few feet seawards, before I regained my feet and stumbled to the safety of the higher rocks.

I continued round the bay, the settlement getting steadily closer. Eventually I reached sand, and then I was walking along a ledge of flat black rock near the sea, with lower black cliffs on my left side. The rock was very slippery, but apart from that it was easy to walk on. I came round a bend and there, suddenly, was a group of people, men and women, walking along the rocks towards me. I realised that they were from the settlement and they had seen me.

I could hardly believe it. After all my troubles I was safe. I let out a cry and started to run. Jumping from rock to rock, waving my arms, so close to the people that I could make out their individual features, hearing but not registering their shouts of 'Careful, lad!' and 'Watch out!', and forgetting in my exultation the slippery seaweed underfoot, forgetting that is, until my feet went from under me, there was a violent pain in my head and a flash of light, and then nothing.

***

Jack has asked me to relate what I know about the next few hours. I don't know if I can contribute much, but I can see his point that if I didn't there'd be a gap in his story. My name's Elizabeth, and I come from Kimmeridge Bay.

We aren't bad people, despite what's said about us. The fishing's hard at Kimmeridge, no shelter at all really, so it's quite natural that we supplement our income with some free trading when the opportunity arises, which it does quite often. It's not our fault if people are so keen to have brandy and tea and other fine goods but don't want to pay the government's price.

The same goes for the wrecking. The exposed coast that makes the fishing bad means that sometimes an unlucky ship or its wreckage ends up on the ledges off our beach. Not as many as you might imagine, for they mostly make it up Channel if they've escaped Lyme Bay. The law says the wreckage belongs to the King, but he doesn't need it as much as we do, and he's not here either. We take the view that it's finders keepers. We never set out to lure the ships ashore, as it's said they do in Cornwall and such like godless places, but if the sea provides we accept the gift. Sometimes men as well as ships are washed up on the beach, but we always treat them properly, and our men have often taken risks to rescue poor seafarers.

It's not just the sea that provides our living. Some of the men walk along the coast to work in the quarries at Worth or Portland, and some dig out shale from the cliffs to sell for people to burn in their fires. With one thing and another, we get along.

That night in August was very stormy, and at first light men went out along the cliffs to see what might be ashore. There was great excitement when Sam came running back saying that there was a lot of wood and bales towards Edgecombe. A good party of us set out, everyone that was in the place really, women and children as well. We had just got outside when we saw a figure walking along the beach from the west. Thinking that he might be a sailor from a ship gone ashore, we walked towards him.

The rocks of Kimmeridge are treacherous underfoot when the tide's out, and when we saw him break into sort of a run we shouted for him to look out, but he took no notice and jumped from rock to rock, waving his arms and shouting. Well, it wasn't long before the inevitable happened, and he fell over very heavily, hitting his head so hard on the rock that I could hear the noise twenty yards away, over the wind and the sea.

He lay still and several of us were sure he was dead, but Nancy bent her head close to his and announced that he was breathing. He was only a lad, about my age, and the men took it in turns to carry him back. He was taken into our house, and laid on a bed in front of the fire. My mother and aunt undressed him and covered him up with blankets. His right hand was badly hurt, there was a huge bruise on his head, and there were small cuts and bruises all over him. They put bandages on his hand and head, and tried to get him to swallow some brandy but couldn't, he was completely out cold.

There was great impatience to get along the coast to the wreck, so I was told to stay and look after him. I was worried by this task, as I thought that he might die if I did the wrong thing, but my mother assured me that all we could do was keep him warm and hope for the best. Nevertheless, for the first hour or so I leaned close to him every few minutes to hear his breath. Gradually, as the day went on, some colour came back into his face, his breathing became easier and my checks less frequent.

At about midday, the people came back from the wreck, bent double under the weight of the goods they had found. Though most of the cargo was damaged, there was a considerable quantity of tubs of butter in good condition and a lot of timber. There was happy chatter, and it was decided that another expedition should be mounted that evening when the tide would be low, as there is always concern at these times that some figure in authority might appear and try to take the wreck for himself.

The men set off in the gathering night, lanterns swinging, and I was left alone again with the shipwrecked sailor. By this time he was moving fitfully and sometimes talking to himself, but I could not make out what he was saying, though it was definitely English. I mopped his brow and tried to get him to take some brandy. He had a pleasant face, and I felt very sorry for him.

I sat at the table, mending his clothes by the light of the fire and a lamp, when I heard a noise and looked up. The sailor was standing at the end of the table, supporting himself with a hand upon it. His lips were moving but he was not talking properly. I pushed him back over to the bed and he sat on it. I wrapped the blankets round his shoulders and gave him some brandy, which he swallowed this time, and then some water.

'My head hurts,' was the first thing he said, more of a groan, really.

'I'm not surprised,' I replied, 'you hit it very hard on the rock.'

'How long have I been here?' he asked

'Since this morning, and it's now about nine.'

'How can I get to Weymouth?' he asked, in great agitation.

'By walking, of course. Sea's too high to go by boat today.'

'Is there a magistrate or somebody near here?'

'No, we try not to have too much to do with people like that, we prefer to go our own way.'

'Is your father here?'

'No, everybody's away at the wreck.'

'What wreck's that, my boat?'

'If your boat was a big ketch carrying butter it was.'

'No, it was a small French fishing boat.' His voice was slurred, and although his eyes were bloodshot they were staring at me with uncommon intensity. I thought that perhaps his ordeal had made him a bit mad.

'What were you doing on a French fishing boat?' I asked. I was burning with curiosity, but I also knew my duty. 'You must have some food. I've made some soup. Have some and you'll feel better.'

I guided him over to the table and sat him at a chair. I put soup and a spoon in front of him, but when he tried to eat his left hand shook, and I spooned the food into his mouth. After a few mouthfuls he turned his head away, and would eat no more. He looked terrible, but there was an urgent and eager look about him.

'I've got to get to Weymouth.'

'You can't go anywhere at the moment, you're very sick with that bang on the head. It'll take days to get better. I remember when my father hit his head a couple of years ago mother made him stay in bed for three days, and she always says now that it wasn't long enough, and your hand's bad, too.'

He felt the back of his head gingerly and looked down at his bandaged hand. He looked so ill that I thought he was going to faint.

'I've got to warn the King. The Frenchies will get him and invade us if I don't.'

He stared at me, and I wondered what to do. It was as I had suspected, his ordeal had made him mad. If he hadn't been so weak I would have been quite worried, but he didn't look threatening, and indeed I had to admit that he was quite comely.

He stood up, swaying. 'I've got to go, don't you understand? It's important.'

'You can't go anywhere, especially with no clothes on!'

He looked down and realised that he was naked, but even this did not seem to deter him. I thought I had better keep him talking to distract him, as I was sure that he was incapable of walking to the door, never mind Weymouth.

'Tell me why you must get to Weymouth. What's all this about the King and the Frenchies? Tell me, and then perhaps I can help you. I don't know what you're talking about now.' He'd been dreaming, I was sure of that, and if he started to talk perhaps he would realise his foolishness, and lie back down quietly and get better.

I suppose that he took fifteen minutes or so to tell his story, his speech slurred and sometimes trailing off into silence, but he told it well, intensely, reliving his experiences in his mind. His eyes became round with horror when he related his fight with the Mate, and he radiated pride when he told me how he had cast his ship off from the quay. I began to doubt that he was mad almost as soon as he started, and by the end of the story I was sure that everything he had told me was true.

When he finished he looked at me and said, 'You see, I must get to Weymouth. I must go now and warn them. The Frenchies might be there tomorrow morning, if they haven't done the job already. Please give me my clothes and I must go.'

He couldn't go. There was no possibility of him being able to walk to Weymouth. It was fourteen miles at least and very hilly.

'You can't go, you just won't make it.'

'When will your father be back?'

'Probably not till morning. It's a fine night. They'll have a big fire going on the beach and they'll stay there for the night, especially if there was drink on the ship.'

He gave a despairing look and then got up and reached across to the table for his clothes, but overbalanced and just managed to sit on a chair rather than collapse.

'See what I mean, you can't go anywhere.'

He held his head in his hands. 'But we must warn them. What about the boat?'

'The surf's too high, we'd never launch it.' A sudden thought came into my head. 'I can walk there, I'll go. I've been there lots of times and I know the way.'

He looked at me, relief flooding into him, and started to speak. Then he seemed to have further thoughts and his face clouded. 'But you can't, you're a girl.'

'Well, it seems to be me or nobody,' I said, and in truth I

124

have always been keen to have adventures and could hardly contain my enthusiasm. He looked doubtful but realised that there was no other option.

I thought quickly, not of the walk over the hills, for I had done that before and knew the way, but of what I should do when I got there.

'Who shall I see in Weymouth? Do you know anybody important there who could warn the King?'

He looked perplexed but then brightened. 'Mrs Wellstead, that's who. She must know people who can tell the King. I'll write a letter for her. Have you got pen and paper? Can you write?'

We had, and I could, though I think that my family was the only literate one in Kimmeridge Bay. I got out the pen and a sheet of paper and wrote as he spoke in a low hesitant voice:

Mrs Wellstead,
The Cicely was taken by the French because of the treachery of Dennis Vasey. Your husband is a prisoner with the crew in France, but they are all well. I escaped and am now at Kimmeridge Bay, hurt. This letter is being carried by ...

He looked at me enquiringly.
'Elizabeth Brown,' I said.

Elizabeth Brown, who rescued me from the sea. The French intend to use the Cicely to bring soldiers into Weymouth and capture the King off the esplanade. They will seize Weymouth and invade England. You must warn the King so that he can escape. Please act quickly as the ship may arrive at any time.

Jack Stone
Apprentice to Mr Wellstead

The effort of composing the letter had exhausted him, and I guided him back to the bed and laid him down on it. I ate

125

some soup, banked up the fire and put on my coat. No time to waste. At the door I glanced back. Jack was lying on the bed, watching me.

'Best of luck, Elizabeth,' he called, softly, and I went through the door out into the night.

Chapter 14
Weymouth

Though I should probably say that I was motivated that night solely by duty, in truth I was not. I was young and the prospect of adventure exhilarated me.

I believe, that measured on a map, the distance between Kimmeridge Bay and Weymouth is fourteen miles or so, but that doesn't take into account the vertical distance you have to travel if you actually make the journey. There is a path along the coast, well worn and easy to follow, but it constantly climbs up and down hills, making the journey seem longer than it actually is. I had walked the route several times before. The night was fine and I was used to being out in the dark and not frightened of it. I was accustomed to walking long distances and the journey presented no particular difficulties to me.

I walked steadily past Flowers Barrow, Worbarrow, Arish Mell, Mupe, Lulworth, Dordle Dor, White Nothe, Ringstead, Osmington and Redcliff. As it got light and I could see down into the yellow curve of Weymouth Bay I began to get anxious. Could one of those ships be the *Cicely*, full of Frenchmen? I walked quickly, eventually breaking into a run.

Despite the early hour the town's streets were busy and the shops open. It did not seem to me as if the French had already arrived. I could see two warships in the bay and knew that they were the ones Jack had told me about, guarding the King. I looked anxiously around the bay for the *Cicely* but could not see any ship that resembled what I thought she might look like.

With some difficulty, after asking several people, I found Wellstead's house. It seemed very grand and I was somewhat overawed. I went up to the front door and knocked on it as loud as I could. There was no response. I knocked again and again, but nothing happened. I looked in through a bay window and saw expensive-looking furniture and carpets, but the house did not look lived in. I sat on the step and wondered what to do. During my long trip in the night I had been anticipating the moment when I handed the letter over to Mrs Wellstead, imagining her reaction to its contents, expecting her to march out immediately to warn the Army or Navy. I gave hardly any consideration to her likely reaction to the news contained in the letter that her husband and his ship had been captured by the French. In retrospect I am glad that I was not the bearer of this news. The King must be warned, but how? The story somehow seemed less believable here in Weymouth in daylight. I had to get to somebody who would listen to me.

I looked up from these thoughts and realised that I was at the seafront and that the King was not far away, surrounded by an amazing collection of people bowing and elbowing each other, just as Jack had described. The King was not at all impressive, dressed plainly and carrying a walking stick. He had no guard as far as I could see. I was overcome with anxiety. Here he was, right by the sea, and the French might be coming at any moment to snatch him. The throng of people was advancing in my direction. They were all so intent on their own business that they took no notice of me. I might have been invisible as the crowd flowed past me, though I was jostled and bumped. Before I really had time to think I was only a few feet from the King, and I started to rush towards him, reaching for the letter in my pocket.

'Sir, Sir,' I heard my voice shouting, and the King and the men and women round him turned in my direction. I was within three feet, waving the letter, when one of the men caught me and held me in strong arms.

My voice was high, almost unrecognisable. 'Let me go, it's important, I must give the King this letter. It's dangerous here, the French are coming to get him!'

Suddenly the King was staring at me, his mouth open, looking surprised, and the man who was holding me snatched the letter from my hand. He read it quickly, grabbed my arm and with his other arm was pushing the King, shouting 'Make way, make way!' as we went up a road away from the shore, with the King stumbling in front. For a hundred yards or so we went, the crowd following us at a distance, looking at the scene with startled eyes. The man holding me turned to the crowd and shouted 'Get Colonel Corner', and a man ran off to do his bidding.

We got to a large house and went up the steps, the King almost tripping and looking confused. There were red-coated soldiers at the door, and the man holding me shouted 'French attack, guard the doors' as we went past, and I heard the doors shut and saw the soldiers kneel by the door, shouldering their muskets. We ran up wide stairs, into a large room with chairs and a desk. The King sat heavily on a chair, and the man who had read the letter released me. My wrist hurt where he had been holding me.

By now I was feeling frightened and confused. I had expected that the King's men would be difficult to convince of the truth of my story, but I could see that they were taking it seriously. A man ran into the room, his face as red as his uniform coat. I presumed that it was Colonel Corner.

'Your Majesty,' he began, but the man who had grabbed me put his arm up to silence him and handed him the letter. The Colonel read it quickly, his face becoming even redder.

'I see,' he said, when he had finished. At that moment another man in naval uniform burst into the room. Colonel Corner, nodding his head, said 'Captain Martin, good day' and handed him the letter.

When Captain Martin had read the letter, he and the other officer looked at my captor. 'Your Grace,' said the naval man, 'how did you come by this letter?'

Your Grace? I had been captured by somebody very

important! I later learned he was the Duke of Clarence, the King's son, later to become William IV. He didn't look very grand to me, middle aged and burly, more like a fisherman really if the truth was told.

They turned to me. 'Well, out with it, girl,' said the Duke gently.

I related as much as I could remember of what Jack had told me. When I had finished they discussed what I had said, and I caught snatches of conversation.

'Morlaix, eh? Might have expected it.'

'Boney's scheme, you may depend on it.'

'The *Waterwitch*. He's a keen man, that Watts, d' ye know him?'

'Get him away. Dorchester, he'll be safe enough there.'

'We'll have to recognise the *Cicely*, though, all depends on that.'

The King took almost no part in these discussions, but beckoned me to go over to him. To my surprise he took my hand, looked me in the eye and asked me my name. He seemed a pleasant, kind man. He asked me where I lived and what my family did, and about Jack Stone. I told him as much as I could, but our conversation was interrupted by the arrival in the room of yet another officer, accompanied by several troopers who took the King away. As he left he patted my hand and then waved.

More officers arrived and orders were given. I could hear running and shouting in the streets. The Duke turned and said, 'Come with me,' and I followed him and Captain Martin as they walked briskly out of the house and down the street to the esplanade. A naval pinnace was drawn up on the beach. As we approached, the sailors launched her, and to my amazement the Duke picked me up, carried me through the surf and put me in the boat.

The sailors, finely attired with straw hats and ribbons, rowed fast out to one of the frigates, resplendent in yellow and black paint. The frigate was familiar to me, as it frequently passed close to Kimmeridge, taking Royal visitors on excursions from Weymouth. As we came alongside I could see sailors running with bare feet on the decks and heard orders being shouted. We went up the accommodation ladder, accompanied by the piercing noise of a whistle. The Captain and the Duke turned to the stern of the ship and saluted, and I was taken by a uniformed sailor into a cabin in the stern with large windows.

I heard the click of the capstan pawl and the ship heeled as sail was got on her. I saw the coastline pass and realised that we were retracing my path of the night before along the coast, the ship sailing fast with a great wake behind her. The man in uniform brought me some food, which I ate hungrily for I had not had anything since the night before. Almost as soon as I had finished I heard orders given, and the ship came upright as sail was reduced. We went slowly in towards the land and the leadsman sang out the depth. The anchor was dropped some distance away from the beach, for Kimmeridge Bay is shallow and there are isolated rocks to trap the unwary. I was led out of the cabin as the boat, which had been towing astern, was brought alongside. Everything on that ship seemed to be done with great calmness, there was hardly any shouting.

The pipes sang out again as I was led down the ladder by the Duke, with Captain Martin following. I sat in the stern with them as a young man steered. He asked me where to land and I pointed to the spot near the slipway. I could see people waiting outside their houses and knew that they would be worried at this approach of authority. The boat grounded and Captain Martin and the Duke, accompanied by another naval officer, got out into the surf, which was quite heavy, as sailors held the boat. I was standing up about to get out myself when the Duke picked me up and carried me the few yards to the beach. As he put me down, my father came forward, his cap in his hand. If father was surprised to see me carried ashore by a Duke he did not show it. I hugged him and turned as the Duke said to me. 'Where is he?' I knew that he meant Jack.

I pointed to our house, 'Over here, sir,' and led the way across the slipway. My mother was tending the fire but straightened as we entered, and I could see Jack sitting at the table, looking much recovered. As he saw me his face broke into a smile, and then he looked at the men with me.

'Jack,' I said, 'this is Duke William, and this is Captain Martin.' I didn't refer to the other officer who was with them as I didn't know his name. 'The King's safe at Dorchester, and the French haven't landed yet.'

The three men sat at the table and looked at Jack, who was by now grinning broadly and, though he might not like me saying so, looking rather silly. The events of the day had taken such an astonishing turn that by now introducing Duke William to a shipwrecked mariner in my own cottage did not seem unusual. I heard my mother saying 'Tea, sirs?', and briefly wondered if we would get into trouble as I doubted if the King had had his due from the tea in our house.

The Captain said, 'I hear you've a remarkable story to tell, young man,' and then they were asking him questions, one after the other, hardly waiting for him to finish before they asked another. Several times during the questioning the men looked at each other with raised eyebrows, and there were several muttered 'Well dones' at various parts of the story. My mother's tea was received and drunk, rather noisily I thought. The tale of how Jack had cut out the *Cicely* was particularly well received, the part about the building on the bowsprit leading to boisterous laughter and spirited speculation about what the Frenchies might have said when he saw the sight in the morning. When the fight with the Mate was related the Duke went so far as to lean over the table and give Jack a hearty slap on the shoulder, muttering 'Sorry' when he saw the look of pain on Jack's face.

When they had finished questioning Jack, Captain Martin took out a watch and declared, 'There's no doubt at all. Off to Poole I reckon, and get word to Pompey for reinforcements.' He looked at Jack. 'We need somebody in the ship who can recognise the *Cicely*. Are you up to it, lad?' I was surprised by the disappointment I felt when Jack said that he was ready to go.

The men got up with Jack, and my father, who had been standing at the back of the room, opened the door for them. I think that he was relieved to have them out of the house. The Duke turned to me and said, 'Thank you very much, Elizabeth, you have done a notable service, and you will hear from us.' He shook my hand, as did Captain Martin and the other officer. Jack looked at me and said 'Thank you' and then they got into the boat and were gone, leaving me disconsolate on the beach.

***

I felt rather dazed when Lizzie's father and mother returned that morning after their expedition to the wreck, waking me from a deep sleep. My head ached and there was a dull throb in my injured hand, but I was definitely improving.

The questions began when they saw that Lizzie was not there. For a moment I could not remember what had happened the previous night, but gradually my memory returned. They were not pleased that Lizzie had gone off to Weymouth, but they had great faith in her and were not very much worried for her safety. Despite this they decided that someone should go to Weymouth to meet her, and an uncle was dispatched along the coast path, as her father had a twisted leg as a result of a fishing accident.

I was given more soup, which I was able to eat, and I spent the morning sleeping by the fire. At midday I got up and put my clothes on.

There was considerable excitement when a ship was seen approaching, and when I heard that it was a frigate I hoped that its visit was the result of Lizzie's trip to Weymouth. Even so, when I saw her come into the house with the three officers I could hardly believe my eyes. She had done it! My astonishment was complete when she introduced one of the men as Duke William, the King's son. They questioned me closely and at the end decided their frigate should go to Poole so that a dispatch could be sent to Portsmouth, requesting reinforcements and acquainting the Admiralty with the situation. They asked me to come on board and I was glad to comply with this request, though I felt a pang of regret when I said goodbye to Lizzie.

I felt weak as soon as I got out of the house. I must have staggered slightly because Captain Martin put his arm round me and supported me as I walked to the boat. As I got near it, sailors in straw hats with ribbons in them came forward and helped me into the sternsheets. The men got into the boat, which was under the command of a young man, and rowed it towards the frigate faster than any boat I had seen rowed before.

By the time we came up with her she was lying hove to with her topsails against the mast and the anchor dripping at the cathead. As we went past her stern I glanced up at the name and stiffened as I saw *Iroise* picked out on her stern in gold letters. Captain Martin saw my surprise and smiled.

'Yes, French built. Captured in '97, fastest frigate in the Navy. Froggie builds a good ship,' he finished reflectively.

I heard pipes screech as we went on board and watched as the officers turned to the stern of the ship and saluted. The gesture suddenly brought back Morlaix's gesture when he had boarded the *Cicely* that night in Wapping. As I was taken below to where the surgeon worked, I felt the ship heel as sail was crowded on. The surgeon, a man of few words but great skill, inspected my wounds and expertly bandaged them, putting splints on the fingers he thought might be broken.

When he had finished he said in what I later knew to be a Scotch accent, 'You're a lucky young man, that's a nasty wound you've got there on your head. A little bit harder and you'd never have woken up. A week or so of rest, though, and you'll be right as rain.'

He turned and indicated a thin young man who was standing behind me. I suppose he was seventeen years or so old and I recognised him as the commander of the pinnace. 'This is Mr Midshipman Badcock. He'll be looking after you during your stay on our ship.'

Then in a stern voice he continued, 'He's to be kept quiet, plenty of rest. No drink and no vigorous activity, do you understand?'

Midshipman Badcock grinned. 'Aye, aye, Mr Surgeon, I'll do exactly as you say.' He put his hand out to me. 'Pleased to meet you, Jack, the whole ship is amazed by you taking on Froggie singlehanded. Watch your head.'

I went with him through the ship, taken aback by the number of men and the amount of equipment on board. Every inch of the ship seemed to be used for something. She was bigger than the *Cicely*, massively built and beautifully kept up. I thought she was not so much a ship, more of a gigantic fighting machine, with everything conducted with an air of quiet efficiency. We went into a cabin where there were four other young men, one not much older than me. I shook hands with them, and then I must have looked rather shaky, for I was led to a settee on which I lay down gratefully.

I was woken by a shake on my shoulder. I peered up at Badcock's face, illuminated by a swinging light. 'Captain Martin wants to see you,' he said. I got up and he gave me a drink of what he claimed was coffee before leading me along the windswept deck aft to the cabin. It was getting dark, the ship was sailing fast and I could see that we were just off Swanage. Badcock led me into a great cabin in the stern, where Captain Martin, the Duke and two other officers were sitting at a polished table.

Captain Martin spoke. 'Jack, we've written an account of what has happened to you which we are about to send ashore for the Admiralty. We would like you to read it and tell us if we have made any mistakes or left out anything important.'

I was given some papers, and then Badcock took me into

another cabin, where I sat and read what had been written. As I finished each page it was eagerly grabbed and read by Badcock, to the accompaniment of low whistles and compliments I waited in dread for the inevitable slap on the shoulder, but was able to forestall it by holding up my hand.

The account that they had written seemed accurate to me, and Badcock led me back to the main cabin. I told the officers there that the report was accurate and they dismissed me. As Badcock led me back to the midshipman's berth, he explained that the pinnace was to take the report to Portsmouth, while the ship returned to guard Weymouth. He was to command the pinnace, and Midshipman Snowden would have charge of me in his absence.

We passed Poole, and the frigate was hove to in gathering darkness off a deserted and desolate-looking shore which Badcock told me was called Bourne Mouth and, with a wink, informed me was a well-known haunt of smugglers. I watched as he got his pinnace ready and, dressed in tarpaulins, boarded it and sailed away into the darkness, the frigate being got under way immediately with impressive smartness.

The south-west wind became lighter as darkness gathered. The ship could not lay Weymouth directly and so set a course as close to the wind as she could, out to sea. Snowden, a youth a little older than me, took me to the midshipman's berth, where he gave me some food and offered me rum, which I refused, remembering the surgeon's warning. After my adventures, during which I had been entirely reliant on my own resources, it came almost as a shock to realise that the frigate had no need of my assistance. I climbed into a hammock and fell asleep.

Snowden woke me, shaking my shoulder. In the dim light of the lamp he indicated the coffee on the table, which I drunk gratefully. It seemed to be the middle of the night and I wondered why I had been woken. I asked Snowden.

'Dawn,' he said. I looked puzzled.

'Most dangerous time of the day, you don't know what's

going to appear out of the night. The ship goes to quarters, guns run out, ready for anything.' As he spoke I could hear the ship coming alive. 'You're wanted on the quarterdeck in case your old ship shows up, come on.' He motioned for me to follow and led the way out of the midshipmen's berth to the quarterdeck. As we crossed the dark deck I could hear and see that the ship was a hive of activity. Men were moving quickly but quietly in the darkness, pulling on ropes, opening ports, running out guns and climbing the rigging, and these movements generated a buzz of noise with occasional clangs of ironwork as the guns were readied.

I arrived on the quarterdeck to find Captain Martin already there, telescope under his arm, accompanied by several officers. They acknowledged me, and I stood near the weather rail, waiting.

Chapter 15
The Cicely Again

As the light increased the deck and rigging of the *Iroise* gradually became more distinct. I was able to make out the land ahead and realised that the ship was slanting into Weymouth Bay, which was five or six miles distant, with the dark bulk of Portland visible on the port bow. The wind was still south-westerly and the frigate was close hauled on the port tack, hissing through the waves with every stitch of canvas set.

There was a hail from the foremast top, a stir of excitement on the quarterdeck, and Captain Martin raised his telescope to his eye.

'Is that her?' he asked, handing me the glass and pointing to a sail fine on the port bow. I took the telescope, focused it and the *Cicely* swam into view. She was perhaps a mile away, innocent and natural in the surroundings of her home port. There she was, my own ship, sailing along off Weymouth, filled with Frenchmen intent on capturing the King. My head injury and tiredness made my mind wander. Had the events of the last week or so been real? I imagined I could see the familiar figure of Wellstead on the *Cicely's* poop, wearing his great coat. That coat, where had it gone? I tried to remember. I'd been wearing it ….

'Well?' I was brought back to reality by the sound of Captain Martin's voice, tense and impatient. For a moment I didn't realise what he meant, then I said, rather indistinctly, 'Yes, sir, that's her.'

The Captain's voice became gentler, as though questioning a child. 'Is that the *Cicely* ahead?'

'Yes, sir, she's got a new foremast, but there's no doubt at all.'

The news caused a ripple of excitement to spread round the ship. Orders were given and the ship was readied for action. Ammunition was placed by the guns, buckets were filled with water, the decks sprinkled with sand, and nets were draped over the bulwarks with the men's hammocks in to reduce the danger of flying wood splinters. The ship's company of marines, resplendent in red coats, was mustered on deck, carrying their long muskets. A huge ensign was hoisted from the mizzen peak to cheers from the men.

As the sails were trimmed and retrimmed, in an attempt to coax more speed out of the Navy's fastest frigate, the men were given breakfast and a tot of rum. I was not told to do anything else, so I stayed on the quarterdeck, watching with fascination and admiration as the frigate's crew went smoothly through the routine of readying their ship for battle.

Captain Martin came over to me and asked about the *Cicely's* armament. I thought that the French had cut six gunports in each side of the ship, but I could not be sure. This information was relayed to the other officers, who were now all wearing their best uniforms. I looked towards the land and saw that the other guard frigate was sailing out from Weymouth on a course to intercept the *Cicely*. The Duke came on deck and I noted in surprise that he was wearing a naval uniform. He walked over to the Captain and they conversed in low tones, with much nodding of heads.

The frigate was considerably faster than the *Cicely* and we were about half a mile distant, overhauling her rapidly. I noticed that she had two boats in tow astern, quite large ones, and assumed that these were intended to take the men ashore for the attempt to capture the King. I thought that by now Morlaix on the *Cicely* must know the game was up, with one frigate on his tail, crowding on sail and with her guns run out, and another coming out to meet him. This was clearly not a routine inspection of a merchant ship, to be brushed off with a few words in English. Morlaix's operation

139

was entirely reliant on surprise, he did not have the means to fight his way into Weymouth. As a naval man he would know that his converted merchant ship was no match for the smooth running engines of destruction that were the British warships.

Any doubts he might have entertained about the frigate's intention were removed a few minutes later when signal flags were hoisted on the frigate's mizzen by Midshipman Snowden's men. I did not know what the flags meant, but I did not think it was '*Bon voyage*'. Their probable meaning was reinforced a few moments later when the frigate's bow chasers fired, doing no discernible damage to the enemy but raising a cheer from the *Iroise's* men.

The frigate was now a few hundred yards behind the *Cicely*, and I reflected that it was a change for the better to see my old ship from the vantage point of a warship's deck, rather than from that of a swimmer, as I seemed to have been done far too frequently. I wondered what Morlaix would do. He seemed to have no avenue of escape and, thinking of all the men in her hold, I hoped that he would strike his colours before the frigate used her broadside. For a moment I thought he was striking, for the red ensign at the *Cicely's* peak was hauled down. I was not the only one under this impression, for a murmur went round the ship, to be silenced immediately as a huge tricouleur was hoisted in its place and the gunports which had been cut in her hull opened and guns were run out. There were six of them on each side as I remembered, but the guns looked small in comparison with the frigate's.

At that moment the *Cicely* went about. With her preponderance of fore and aft sails, in the right hands and conditions, the *Cicely* was remarkably fast in stays and was soon sailing quickly out to sea. Orders were given and the *Iroise* started to tack in response. She was a larger ship than the *Cicely*, square rigged, and she tacked much slower. She was still hanging in irons, bow into the wind, with sailors pulling on ropes to back the forecourse to bring her round when I noticed that the *Cicely* had altered course to pass close ahead of us. I watched amazed as an incredible number of men poured from her hold onto the deck, all carrying muskets. They took up station round the ship, kneeling or standing braced, and many of them slung their muskets over their shoulders and climbed into the rigging.

I suddenly realised what she was going to do. Morlaix had outmanoeuvred Martin, who I think was mentally preparing himself for boarding a merchant ship. Though the *Cicely* had few guns, all of them were trained on the frigate, whose devastating broadside could not be brought to bear until she had tacked. The Duke put it succinctly into words. 'Crossed the T, by God.' The *Iroise* was starting to swing quite quickly now, but though the crew desperately hauled on sheets and braces, there was not enough time. Morlaix had caught us.

The *Cicely* was aiming to pass ahead of us, perhaps fifty yards away. I briefly saw Morlaix standing on the deck near the wheel, and I saw the boats which the *Cicely* was towing released, I presumed to give the ship extra speed in her escape attempt.

The Captain shouted 'Take cover!' and the frigate's men lay behind bulwarks or any available shelter, waiting. The marines dispersed round the ship and I felt a sharp push in my back. It was the Captain. 'Into the cabin, sonny,' he said in a commanding voice. 'Move!'

I needed no further urging and moved, running down from the quarterdeck into the cabin. The transformation there was astonishing. Gone were the bulkheads and furniture. It was now an open gun deck, part of the fighting machine, filled with sailors with scarves round their heads manning cannon. Piles of ammunition stood by each gun and slow matches smouldered, ready to fire the cannon if the flintlocks failed. I pressed myself into a corner, for there was nothing I could do to help. I heard Captain Martin shout 'Starboard battery, fire as your guns bear' and the order being passed on, but I knew that none of the guns could be brought to bear.

Then the *Cicely* fired, the crash of her cannon first, followed by the noise of hundreds of muskets. I was safe enough in my corner of the cabin, though it was frightening to listen to the scream of shot and the thud of balls hitting woodwork, the cries of men and the noise of destruction. For some reason I thought about the boats the *Cicely* had cast adrift, and a fragment of what the Mate had said to me that night on the Cape came into my mind: '… the frigates will be blown to bits.'

Suddenly I realised what was in the boats. I roused myself and rushed onto the deck, shocked at the wreckage of fallen yards and sails blocking my way. The frigate had turned, but not enough, and I heard more shots coming from the *Cicely*, which was now on the port bow of the *Iroise*, sailing fast out to sea. As I ran up the steps to the quarterdeck more wreckage fell from aloft. I heard myself shouting, 'The boats, don't shoot at the boats, gunpowder in the boats!'

The frigate started to fire back at the *Cicely* in a desultory way, as only a few guns could be brought to bear. The scene on the quarterdeck was horrible, as I think that the French musketeers on the *Cicely* had concentrated their fire there. Dead and wounded men were lying on the deck and there was the terrible noise of men in pain. I ran around the deck shouting, 'Don't fire at the boats, gunpowder,' and looked for Captain Martin. I saw him leaning heavily on the starboard taffrail, clutching his arm, which was wounded, watching the *Cicely* as she sailed away with the tricouleur streaming from her peak.

As the frigate turned, more of her guns could bear on the *Cicely* and the firing became more rapid, though the range was widening rapidly. The noise and confusion was incredible, and there was smoke everywhere. As I ran shouting across the quarterdeck the Captain turned towards me. I saw one of the boats about a hundred yards off the starboard bow, sweeping aft as the frigate began to gather way. I pointed and yelled again, 'Gunpowder in the boat!' I saw his eyes widen in alarm.

'Cease fire! Cease fire!' he shouted in a surprisingly loud voice, and the order was relayed round the ship. The noise of the guns stopped and I watched in relief as the frigate passed the French boat, which was covered in a tarpaulin sheet.

'Helm hard up!' he shouted, and the frigate responded and began to widen the gap between herself and the doom-laden boat.

And then one of the frigate's guns fired, followed by another. I think that the gunners, keyed up for action, had suddenly seen a target and had fired automatically. The Captain was screaming 'Cease fire! Cease fire!' as I heard a third gun roar, followed by an unbelievable concussion as the boat's cargo exploded. The frigate heeled as the blast hit her and for a moment the air was filled with flying debris and then deluged in a spray of water thrown up from the explosion.

There was utter and complete silence. Men lay where they had been thrown by the explosion, deafened by its noise and shocked by its violence. The tattered sails flapped in the breeze as the ship lost way and stopped in the water.

Then the training and discipline of the Royal Navy took over. Men formed into parties and went about their allotted tasks. The ship was got under way, slowly, after the *Cicely*. Wounded men walked or were taken below, wrecked spars cut away, and new ropes and sails retrieved from stores and bent on. The pumps were got going, and the Captain sat on a chair on the quarterdeck as a surgeon's mate attended to the wound in his arm. The Duke and First Lieutenant came and stood by him as a succession of tradesmen made their reports. Surgeon, master, carpenter and sailmaker stood in turns in front of the chair listing the damage and taking instructions. The gunner was not present, that department being represented by the gunner's mate.

To his credit, the Duke did not intervene in the running of another man's ship, but from time to time put his hand on the Captain's shoulder in an encouraging gesture. I saw them confer, and Midshipman Snowden, who was standing at a distance which might be construed as respectful but which still allowed him to hear what was going on, was called over and wrote a signal down on his pad, which his men soon hoisted on the mizzen. The signal was acknowledged by the other frigate, which wore round and headed back towards the land. I supposed that the officers had realised that the *Cicely* might not be the only French ship in the attack, and had decided that the other frigate should return and guard Weymouth.

With surprising speed the frigate was restored to sailing trim, and within an hour all of the broken and damaged spars and sails had been replaced. Morlaix had not wasted this opportunity, though, and the *Cicely* was several miles ahead, heeling in the moderate south-westerly breeze and still flying the tricouleur.

The hands were stood down from quarters and given dinner. The action, which had seemed shattering to me, appeared to have little impact on the crew of the frigate and they went about their duty relatively cheerfully. I went down to the midshipmen's berth and gratefully ate the food that was given to me. I was told that the frigate had lost three men in the encounter with the *Cicely*, including the gunner, and that there were a large number of wounded. There was debate about whether the Captain should have tacked when he did, and general admiration for the way the French had fought and handled their ship. Everybody was confident that the *Iroise* would catch the *Cicely* and that the result when she did would be a foregone conclusion. The most lively debate, however, was reserved for the question of prize money, that great motivator of naval men. The *Cicely* was English, stolen by the French. Did that make her a legitimate prize? Various positions were taken and argued with skill and legal knowledge that I had previously imagined was only held by the inhabitants of the Temple.

When I went back on deck, the *Iroise* was living up to her reputation as the best sailing frigate in the Navy, moving fast through the water and rapidly overhauling the *Cicely*. What was obvious, though, was that the *Cicely*, with her fore and aft sails, was more close winded, that is she could sail more directly into the wind than the square rigged frigate. If the frigate was to catch the *Cicely*, she would have to tack, and the moment would have to be judged carefully to avoid putting the frigate into the position she had been in earlier. There was now no lack of respect for the Frenchmen aboard the *Cicely*.

The frigate overtook the *Cicely* about one in the afternoon, probably a mile to leeward of her. The French coast was visible ahead and also a low island, which I was told was Alderney. When the *Iroise* was well ahead, she was tacked round and set on a course to take her across the *Cicely's* bow. As we approached, the frigate's crew was beaten to quarters and the guns run out, the ship's band striking up rousing tunes like 'Lilli Bulero' and 'Heart of Oak', which the crew sung along to with great gusto. I watched as the *Cicely* tacked away from us, not more than a mile off our lee bow. The frigate was overhauling her rapidly and soon her broadside would bear. That would be the end of it I thought, and for the second time that day waited for the *Cicely* to slow and strike her colours. The frigate was close now, heeling, moving quickly, the engine of destruction ready to tear the *Cicely* to pieces. I could see the men on the *Cicely's* deck duck behind bulwarks as our bow chasers came within range and fired.

'Port battery, stand by. Starboard battery, fire as you bear … steady,' shouted the Captain, for the second time that day. This time there was to be no mistake. And then I saw men on the *Cicely* throw barrels over the side, one at a time, barrels that to my amazement started to explode with great violence as the frigate came up to them. Tattered holes appeared in the frigate's sails and I heard shouts and screams from forward. The frigate was hard on the wind and could only alter to starboard to avoid the barrels, but this lost her valuable yards of weather gauge. I saw the Captain standing grim on the quarterdeck as the *Cicely* luffed up into the wind, as though to tack, but the frigate had no intention of becoming the vertical stroke in the T for the second time that day, and the helm was immediately put down and the frigate tacked to follow her.

But the *Cicely* didn't tack. Just as she lost way, her headsails were backed and she fell back onto the port tack. There was much running and heaving of ropes on the *Iroise* as she was eventually brought onto the port tack, but she had lost a lot of ground to the other ship.

The *Cicely* came up into the wind again and this time she did tack, firing her broadside at the frigate but doing no damage. The frigate kept on her course, and when she was broadside on to the *Cicely* she fired, one gun at a time as the gunners carefully sighted their weapons. There was a cheer from the *Iroise's* crew as holes appeared in the *Cicely's* sails, but it seemed to have no effect on her speed.

The duel continued as the afternoon wore on, the frigate unable to get to grips with the *Cicely*, but firing occasional shots. From the frigate's deck I watched an exhibition of ship handling such as I have never seen before or since. Morlaix made use of all the *Cicely's* advantages, and ruthlessly exploited the frigate's weaknesses, I had never seen the *Cicely* handled so well, tacking smartly, hanging in stays, backing and filling, and sailing closer to the wind than the square rigged frigate could. The *Iroise* was handled with skill and smartness, but there was no doubt that Captain Martin, who was suffering considerably from his wound, had met his match in Morlaix.

With each manoeuvre the *Cicely* either gained slightly on the frigate, or got in more towards the French coast. The frigate's officers were almost beside themselves with frustration, and this was increased when we watched in amazement as a long barrelled gun with large wheels was brought onto the *Cicely*'s quarterdeck.

'Field gun,' said one of the midshipmen near me. 'Must have brought it along for the invasion.'

From that time on the field gun kept up a monotonous fire on the frigate, never ceasing despite the wild manoeuvres of the *Cicely*, one shot about every three minutes. It had a depressing and wearying effect on the crew, and though the bow chasers spoke often in reply, it seemed that the merchant ship was getting the best of us.

As the sun went down in the west, the closest point of France, a cape called Cap de la Hague, was only a few miles away, clearly visible. The *Cicely* had tacked towards the land and we had followed, expecting that she would soon tack again. When the *Cicely* had been on the same tack for several minutes, it became clear that she was making a run for it. There was excitement on the frigate as we realised that we would be able to overhaul her if she stayed on this course. The excitement lasted for a few minutes until we saw that the frigate would not weather Cap de la Hague, but that the *Cicely*, with the advantages of a half a mile of weather gauge and her fore and aft rig, would.

Midshipman Snowden arrived next to me, and told me to go to the quarterdeck, wincing as a ball from the *Cicely*'s field gun screamed into the sea a few yards away. Captain Martin was still sitting in his chair, looking strained and pale, with the Duke and several officers round him. He asked me about the *Cicely*'s likely destination and I told him that I thought it would be Carteret, as I did not think there was any naval establishment at the port where I had stolen the fishing boat.

'I don't think she'll get over the bar at Carteret unless it's high tide,' I volunteered, and he nodded in agreement.

'Tide's flooding now,' he said, then 'Ouch' as a ball from the *Cicely*'s field gun screamed towards us and crashed into the frigate's side. 'Set your watch by it,' remarked the First Lieutenant.

The Captain asked me whether I had seen any fortifications at Carteret, and I told him that I had not. By his questions I supposed that they intended to try to catch the *Cicely* as she waited for the tide there.

At that moment there was a hail from the masthead. 'On deck there, sail two points on the starboard bow.' The First Lieutenant raised his telescope and looked in the direction indicated and there was a stir of excitement among the group of officers. 'On deck there, looks like a British frigate, *Waterwitch* or *Sprite* I reckon.'

The First Lieutenant scrambled into the mizzen rigging, carrying his telescope, dignity forgotten. He returned to the quarterdeck panting. 'He's right, it is *Waterwitch*. I'd recognise that foretops'l anywhere, Watts swears by having 'em cut flat.'

The Captain spoke. 'Good man, Watts, real nose for a prize, never lets one go by.' He turned to me. 'Suppose you've had first-hand experience, lad!' There was general laughter.

Then the Duke spoke. 'The field piece has stopped firing.' There was a general realisation that it had, at last.

'She's signalling, sir,' said the First Lieutenant. Midshipman Snowden was busy with 'Popham's' – the code book – and after a pause read out *HM frigate* Waterwitch *to British frigate on my port bow do you wish me to engage merchant ship*?

The Captain spoke to Snowden: 'Make *HM frigate* Iroise *to* Waterwitch *engage enemy exercise caution enemy ship carrying 500 troops.*'

After some delay the requisite flags were hoisted, and Snowden read out the reply. 'Waterwitch makes *Affirmative*, sir.'

'Make *Caution enemy may use floating bombs* and *Caution enemy ship heavily armed.*'

'Waterwitch makes *Affirmative merchant ship is* Cicely *of*

Weymouth spoke Waterwitch *London for Jersey 18 August,* sir.'

'Make Cicely *in hands of enemy.*'

By now the *Cicely* was up to Cap de la Hague close inshore, with the *Waterwitch* sailing to cut her off as she headed down the French coast.

'Frenchman's signalling, sir,' said the First Lieutenant to Captain Martin, looking through his telescope. 'Must be to the land,' and indeed there was a building on the Cap, with a mast in front of it flying flags as though in response.

The *Iroise* had to put in a short tack to clear the Cap, and for a while we were out of sight of the *Cicely*. Then we were past the cape, the *Cicely* in sight again, sailing fast down through the Race of Alderney with the tide under us. The field piece on the *Cicely*'s poop started firing again towards us, but the range was extreme and we did not see the fall of shots. The *Iroise* was rapidly overhauling the *Cicely* as she headed towards a headland that I was told was the Nez de Jobourg, and the *Waterwitch* was coming up on her starboard bow. Not even Morlaix's tricks could save her now. We had her. There could be no escape.

The *Cicely* passed close under the Nez hard on the wind, with the two British frigates pincering her and the rugged cape with waves breaking against its base cutting off her escape to the east. The *Waterwitch* was now in position almost directly in the *Cicely*'s path, perhaps a mile and a half ahead, and she took in sail, waiting for the *Cicely* to come up to her. No escape. But the *Cicely* tacked, heading a little north of west, out to sea. By now we on the *Iroise* were quite close inshore, and Captain Martin lost no time in tacking the ship to follow her round, and I watched the *Waterwitch* simultaneously wear round and crowd on sail.

It was twilight now, and it seemed obvious that the *Cicely* was heading out to sea in an attempt to lose her pursuers in the darkness. It was clear that the gamble would not pay off, though, as she was being rapidly overhauled, the *Waterwitch* having the weather gauge so that Morlaix could not exploit the *Cicely*'s close windedness. I believe we all thought that with the reinforcement of the *Waterwitch* the *Cicely* was finished. Our crew had been at quarters for much of the day and the ship had been worked very hard. Captain Martin was wounded and all day long had had to maintain a high level of concentration, trying to match the genius of Morlaix. Jaded, he was mentally prepared for a swift conclusion. What could Morlaix do? He had put up a valiant fight, but now there were sixty four guns against his twelve, two heavily built warships against his hastily converted merchant ship. He was trapped. He must strike his colours, there was no alternative.

I make these points in an effort to explain what happened next, for Morlaix had no intention of losing us at sea. He was still a dangerous and determined foe, his ship manned by the cream of the French Navy, and it was not he that was falling into a trap, but us.

We were just about to overhaul her, the gunners standing by to fire at extreme cannon range, when the *Cicely*, for perhaps the fiftieth time that day, tacked, heading back in to the land. There were cries of frustration from the officers on the quarterdeck, and the order was given to tack the frigate.

And then, as the frigate hung in stays we saw the *Cicely* alter towards us, surging full and bye with the wind on her starboard quarter and a bone in her teeth, clearly intending to pass close by our bows. Once again we had been caught and were about to become the vertical stroke of Morlaix's T. I saw the *Waterwitch* start to wear round, but she was moving fast and her turn was a wide one.

Captain Martin immediately saw the danger. 'Done it again, damn his eyes,' he muttered, and then loudly 'Belay the tack. Helm up. Bear away again.'

Orders were shouted. Men ran and pulled sheets and braces with bewildering speed, backing sails so that the frigate gathered sternway and the wheel was put hard a port, forcing the stern round.

The Captain shouted, 'Bow chasers fire as you bear. Stand by starboard battery.'

The frigate was now swinging back onto her original tack, but slowly, so slowly, agonisingly slowly. I heard the Captain say softly to his ship 'Come on my love, come on', patting the taffrail as he spoke.

And then the *Cicely* fired, to my surprise, for the range was still long, certainly too far for musketry. But the *Cicely* shot well despite the range, for I felt at least one ball crash into our hull. As she did so she hauled her wind, heeling as she headed towards the shore, the crash of her bow wave clearly audible.

'Starboard battery, fire as your guns bear!'

The frigate's starboard broadside fired, gun by gun, each one carefully aimed as the range was extreme, disappointment mounting on the quarterdeck as the *Cicely* sailed on undamaged. But then success! A cheer went up as the *Cicely*'s mizzen mast collapsed, but it did not seem to make much difference to her speed as she headed towards the shore, out of range of our guns.

'Going to run her ashore,' said the First Lieutenant as we saw a cove open out in the headland.

'*Waterwitch* makes *Caution off-lying rocks*, sir,' reported Midshipman Snowden. It was now quite dark and the cliffs of France seemed frighteningly close. To take the frigate further inshore would have been reckless in the extreme, and Captain Martin reduced sail and headed offshore, the leadsman in the chains calling out the depth as she went and men straining their eyes for breakers, the exhilaration of the chase giving way to anticlimax and tension.

The *Cicely* must have had men aboard who had local knowledge, probably fishermen, because she was weaving a complicated course through the unseen rocks, sailing fast, despite the loss of the mizzen mast which had now been cut away. I watched as the *Cicely*, her decks alive with men, ran onto the beach with such speed that her bow lifted several feet and she heeled and slewed slightly before coming to rest, firmly aground, hardly moving in the surf. The beach was composed of large pebbles, very steep to, and the end of the *Cicely*'s bowsprit was hanging over dry land. We watched as the men on the deck swarmed – there were so many of them it was like watching insects swarm – down ropes from her bows into the surf and ashore, and then up the beach and, though we could not see, presumably up the cliff.

Our frigate was powerless to intervene. With the tidal streams, the onshore wind and the darkness the ship could not be turned to bring her guns to bear, but we heard and saw the *Waterwitch* firing from further offshore. The *Cicely*'s men did not pause in their activities and it was clear that at that range the shooting was futile.

In fifteen minutes or so the *Cicely* was deserted, and darkness almost complete. Then Morlaix played his master stroke. In the darkness we saw a red glow begin where the *Cicely* lay.

'Fired her, by God,' said the Captain.

The mood on the quarterdeck was gloomy as the blaze grew in intensity. Prize money was an important motivation and there was a valuable ship going up in smoke, but the mood lightened considerably as the fire flickered and went out.

'Too hasty, didn't do the job properly,' remarked the Captain.

The British frigates stood offshore, keeping station as near as possible off the Nez de Jobourg in the strong tidal stream. The officers and men were fed and I had my meal in the midshipmen's berth. None of the midshipmen had been hurt in the action, though one of them, Barton, a boy of about fifteen with blond hair, had a bandaged hand. When pressed, he admitted that the injury had not been the result of enemy action but clumsy knifework while cutting up a piece of ham he had bought in Weymouth.

There was lively conversation about the day's events. It was generally thought that Captain Martin had done a good job, but there was frank admiration for the Frenchmen. Anxiety was expressed about the prize on the beach, with some taking the view that the Captain would leave it and others sure that there would be an attempt to retrieve the *Cicely* on the following day. The debate about the *Cicely*'s status as a prize resurfaced, but it was generally considered that it would be better to argue about it with the ship in our possession.

When two of the midshipmen were called to assist with the boats, it was clear that the *Cicely* was not going to be abandoned. Shortly afterwards I was called to the cabin. Sitting at a table covered with the remains of a meal and charts and books were the *Iroise*'s officers, and other officers who I presumed were from the *Waterwitch*. One of them came towards me, quite short and very stout with greying hair, holding out his hand.

'Captain Watts, *Waterwitch*,' he offered with a strong Dorset accent. 'I believe I've made your acquaintance before, Mr Stone, but last time we didn't speak. Mind you, if you insist on sailing around off the coast of France in a French fishing boat, associating with the *Bernadette*, it's not surprising that I put a ball your way.'

I am afraid to relate that I still resented that incident and I felt a surge of anger run through me. I was tempted to say that my association with the French ketch was not voluntary, but I did not. I was too weary to think of a witty reply and instead mumbled, 'Pleased to meet you, sir. Did you catch her?'

'No we didn't, by God. Played us a merry dance round the Ecrehous, and then off to windward like a rat up a drainpipe. Still, we'll get her one day.'

Captain Martin spoke. He looked much recovered. 'Jack, we're going to take a leaf out of your book and cut out the

Cicely in the morning. Morlaix's tried to burn her and we're going to get her back before he can do the job properly.' There was a murmur of approval from around the table. 'Captain Watts's crew will make up the boarding party. We won't be sending you, I think you've done enough, but we need information about the *Cicely* so that we can get her moving quickly.'

To tell the truth I was glad that I was not to be involved with the boarding. I think by then I had had enough action and fighting. The sight of the dead and wounded on the frigate that day had had a considerable effect on me, my head and hand throbbed and all I wanted to do was sleep.

They asked me questions about the *Cicely*. The pumps, the capstan, where sails were stowed, how much she drew and so on. When they had finished I was given a plate of food by a steward and sat in the corner eating it while the discussions continued. When the officers stood up with their plan decided I was dismissed and went gratefully back to the midshipmen's berth.

Chapter 16
The Prize

Snowden woke me the next morning, telling me that my station was to be with him near the signal halyards. 'Captain wants you handy in case there are any questions about the merchant ship.'

I went on deck to a bright sunny day with a light south-westerly wind. The *Iroise* was half a mile or so off the beach, stemming the tide under reduced sail, and the *Waterwitch* was anchored close inshore. There were three boats alongside the *Waterwitch*, two of her own and one from the *Iroise*. The *Cicely* was lying on the beach, still with her sails up, as she had the previous night. There was no sign of damage to her. In the night the ships' boats had been busy and I could see buoys bobbing in the water marking rocks. I knew that the plan was to anchor the *Waterwitch* as close in as possible, and then use her capstan to pull the *Cicely* off the beach at high tide. The *Iroise* was to stay hove to further off, ready to render assistance if required. High tide would be at about ten o'clock, but there was concern that that morning's tide would not be quite as high as last night's and the *Cicely* would not come off easily. The discussions I had heard last night had focused on the technical difficulties of the salvage operation. There was hardly any discussion about the possibility of enemy action. The *Cicely* had been chased ashore, an attempt had been made to set her on fire and now the Royal Navy was going to claim its prize.

The boats left the *Waterwitch*, two crowded with men and the other towing what seamen refer to as a grass line. These ropes are not actually made from grass but from the coir fibres which cover coconuts. They are used in this type of operation because they float, unlike lines made of sisal or hemp. The grass line was a messenger for a heavy cable made fast aboard the *Waterwitch*. The boats were perhaps a hundred and fifty yards from the *Cicely*, moving quite quickly towards her, when I saw a figure climb down from her bow and make his way over the rough pebbles that made up the beach. I would not say his walk was leisured, but there was no hint of panic about it. I recognised that figure – Morlaix. My stomach churned. They must be planning something.

I turned to Snowden who was also watching the *Cicely* and said, 'That's Captain Morlaix going up the beach.'

We watched as he reached a curve in the cliff and disappeared. Snowden thought quickly. 'I'd better go and tell the Captain.' He ran quickly up onto the quarterdeck, and seconds later came running down, shouting to the seaman at the halyards 'Hoist the recall, quick.'

As the seaman hoisted the signal which was already bent onto the halyard, a gun fired on the *Iroise* and I saw the boats turn and head back towards the anchored ship, the rowers pulling hard at their oars. In the bright sunshine the scene was vivid and colourful, seemingly devoid of menace. I watched as the rowers pulled away from the shore and the *Waterwitch's* crew walked round the capstan, raising the anchor.

And then Hell came to the Nez de Jobourg. We were in Morlaix's trap. Not quite as deeply as he had wished or planned, but in it nevertheless. With a devastating roar the *Cicely* exploded. There was a huge sheet of flame and parts of her flew into the air. I think my ears still ring from the sound of it today, fifty years later. The sea around her turned white with the impact of debris flung into it, and debris continued to fall for what seemed like minutes. The masts with sails still attached rose vertically into the air and then pitched down onto the beach.

Explosions are often described as shattering, and this one was certainly in that category. The *Cicely*, the ship on which I had pinned all my hopes, had ceased to exist. She had literally shattered into pieces. The largest piece was the bottom of the hull, the aft part swept by waves, the forward part burning fiercely. Other parts of the shattered hull lay in the water or on the beach, none of them recognisable parts of a ship. Order into chaos.

The high cliffs round the cove were suddenly covered with men, pulling field guns at incredible speed, their wheels leaping high in the air as they hit bumps. Other men pulled carts which I knew would be piled with ammunition. The guns stopped, and within what seemed like seconds they were firing. Firing and firing, enfilading the poor frigate and the boats. I saw splashes all around the boats, but miraculously they kept rowing, the men ashore concentrating on the bigger prize, the *Waterwitch*. The men on the *Waterwitch* were heaving the capstan round and sail was being made when, suddenly, the gunners ashore found their mark. As though they were corn cut by a scythe, the masts went by the board, sending men on the yards screaming into the sea. And still the firing continued. I watched horrified as men fell on the deck of the *Waterwitch*, wounded or dead. Slowly, after the shock of the ambush, the frigate found her voice and began to fire back. Rock shards screamed from the cliff face as her gunners strove to find enough elevation to strike back.

There are men who can turn certain defeat into victory by their daring and resourcefulness, the breadth of their vision and their ability to inspire their followers and superiors. It has been fashionable recently to ascribe these qualities solely to Englishmen, and God knows we have been fortunate to have had our share of such men. But the truth is that we do not have a monopoly, and the evil genius of Napoleon showed that the French nation is capable of producing fearsome leaders. I consider that it had been the misfortune of Captain Martin to come up against a man, Morlaix, who was simply far removed from the ordinary mould. Perhaps a Drake, a Cochrane or a Nelson could have opposed and outwitted him, but it simply was not possible for an ordinarily talented captain like Martin.

Now the *Iroise* was returning fire with her starboard battery, bow chasers and swivels, at least making the enemy gunners realise that they were not to shoot undisturbed. However, accurate gunnery is much easier from a rocky headland than from a ship which rolls, pitches and changes course. It is the received wisdom that ships cannot successfully engage shore batteries, and our experience that day reinforced that wisdom. Under the sustained fire of the field pieces, the *Waterwitch* began to disintegrate. We watched horror-struck as the men at the capstan were either swept away by shot or decided that they were doing no good in their exposed position and retired below. The ship was a hulk, and I began to suspect that she was settling lower in the water.

The hero of that day was without doubt John Snaith, Master's Mate of the *Iroise,* a man of sixty years or so who was in charge of the frigate's boat. Seeing that the *Waterwitch* would be unable to move herself, he continued rowing past her towards the *Iroise,* the boat still towing the grass messenger line, stopping only when the line was fully paid out. Martin may have been outclassed by Morlaix, but he was still a highly competent seaman and he saw what Snaith was doing. The *Iroise's* helm was put up and she was sailed towards the shore, weaving her way through the buoys marking the rocks.

Soon the *Iroise's* guns could not be elevated sufficiently to engage the enemy on the cliffs above, and word was passed that all men not engaged in working the ship should go below. I do not know why I ignored this order, but I think I was too numb to do anything, and stayed with Snowden and his seamen at the signal halyards.

With consummate skill Martin worked his ship towards the boat towing the grass line, but as he did so the enemy gunners on the cliffs turned their attention to the *Iroise* and, as they found their mark, shot whistled around the ship. Great holes appeared in the sails.

'Chain shot,' shouted Snowden in my ear. 'Trying to cut the rigging.'

For what seemed like an eternity the *Iroise* stood in towards the boat, ghosting along in the light breeze with shot falling all about her. Balls crashed into woodwork sending splinters screaming, until it seemed as though the air was thick with missiles. Those men not under cover below crouched behind bulwarks and any available shelter, but men were hit and taken below.

I watched the crew of the swivels methodically loading, cleaning and carefully aiming their weapons, the long hours of drill paying off. They had the range now, and I watched men on the clifftop drop by the guns and take cover as the grapeshot whined about them. The men at the *Waterwitch*'s swivels, as though encouraged by the approach of the *Iroise*, redoubled their efforts, and the combined fire of the two ships made the fire from the clifftop less effective and slower.

Snowden hoisted *Iroise will take Waterwitch in tow cut your cable at my signal*, but there was no acknowledgement as the *Waterwitch* had no mast from which to hoist signals. We passed the boat and stood on.

'Stand by to wear ship!' roared the Captain and then 'Helm up!' This was a manoeuvre that had to be judged and executed with the utmost precision. Any mistake would place the *Iroise* too far down wind to reach the boat, and the task was complicated by the presence of rocks and the tidal stream running parallel to the beach. Men ran on the decks, ignoring the fall of shot. The frigate slowly came round, close to the cliffs, and headed out to sea again. It was clear that the Captain, pacing the quarterdeck with the First Lieutenant beside him as though taking exercise in Weymouth Bay, had judged his move to perfection, and men stood by for the moment we reached the boat, ready to assist the boat's crew up the side of the ship and take the grass messenger rope.

I watched with astonishment as there was a flat bang from

the clifftop and a barrel-like object flew in a high arc over the bay into the water ahead of the *Iroise*, where it exploded with a loud noise, sending up a fountain of water.

'Siege mortar,' commented Snowden, matter of factly.

The next mortar shell landed astern of us, but closer, and some of the shot which must have been packed in it hit the frigate's hull.

'Bracketed us,' said Snowden. 'Be close next time.'

The siege mortar was invisible from the ship. The enemy had taken advantage of its high trajectory to locate it well inland, shielded from the ships' guns. I saw the First Lieutenant peer intently through his telescope at the cliff and then walk over to the port swivel and speak to its crew, pointing as he did.

'He's seen the spotter,' said Snowden as the swivel fired. I did not see the result of the shot, but the next mortar shell fell harmlessly astern of the frigate.

The *Iroise* came up to the boat and her sails were backed to stop her. Men swarmed up the sides of the frigate from the boat, bringing the grass line with them. The *Iroise's* crew tailed on the grass line, pulling the heavy towing cable through the water to the frigate. I think the gunners on the shore must have realised that their prey could escape, for their rate of fire increased and the shells of the siege mortar started to fall again. The towing cable was made fast round the mizzen mast base and the frigate got under way. We were about a hundred yards from the ruin of the *Waterwitch* when the cable started to tighten, but the *Iroise* had swung slightly as she had waited and the cable had sunk and become caught under the ship's rudder.

The frigate's sails were backed again and, in a display of cool courage which I have never seen equalled, Snaith and his crew got back into their boat and, with shot raining down on them, freed the cable from the rudder. By that time the *Iroise* had swung round almost parallel to the bay and was hazardously close to a group of buoyed rocks. While this was extremely dangerous to the ship, it did give the broadside guns the opportunity to fire at the shore battery, and the fire from there reduced again.

In the light breeze the ship took an agonisingly long time to swing round and start to make way, but at last the cable tightened, and the *Waterwitch* cut her anchor cable as she started to move after the *Iroise*, slowly but surely distancing herself from the shore gunners, whose fire became less and less accurate with every yard gained. It was over with dramatic suddenness. The ships got into the north-going tidal stream, and within minutes the cursed Nez de Jobourg dropped astern, the guns on it silent.

The ebbing tide carried our sad convoy quickly up the coast of France to Cap de la Hague, where we headed out into the Channel. The wind increased to a moderate westerly and the *Iroise*, towing the *Waterwitch*, made surprisingly good progress despite her tattered sails. We stopped the ship shortly afterwards, and the Duke, accompanied by the First Lieutenant, was taken over to the *Waterwitch* to inspect her.

The ship's company was stood down and given dinner. The faces of the midshipmen as they ate were white and shocked. We had lost fifteen men and it was said that the sickbay was crowded with wounded. The ship was badly holed, her sails tattered and the rigging in a dreadful state. There was great admiration for the way Captain Martin had handled the ship, but the greatest praise was for Master's Mate Snaith. There was sombre speculation about conditions on the *Waterwitch*. Captain Watts had been killed along with most of the officers, and it was said that there were 30 dead aboard and a huge number of wounded.

The dinner and rum had a beneficial effect on my companions, but the midshipmen were quiet company and some sobbed quietly in reaction to what they had gone through. After dinner all hands turned to, for there was much work to be done. The ship had to be pumped continuously, for she was leaking badly, and ropes, rigging and sails replaced. I worked where I could be useful with my broken hand. Gradually the ship was got back into working order, though the leak could not be found. As the *Iroise's* condition improved, attention turned to the *Waterwitch*, which was gradually sinking lower in the water. Her crew had rigged a stumpy jury mast, and signals were exchanged between the two ships.

At about five o'clock, the two ships were brought alongside each other and, despite the sea that was running, lashed tightly together, with large fenders between them. Close to, the *Waterwitch* was a dreadful sight, a mastless hulk, low in the water, with jagged holes in the woodwork of her decks and bulwarks. It seemed that almost every part of her was damaged or scarred in some way, and I wondered how any soft-fleshed creature could have survived in that hell of screaming shot and splinters.

A surprisingly large number had survived, but their appearance was shocking, more shocking than the damage to the ship. Many just stood motionless, staring at the *Iroise*, their faces gaunt and white. Those that were working moved listlessly, as though they had lost interest in their own fate. The continuous clanking of the ships' pumps heightened the feeling of desolation. The contrast between the *Waterwitch's* condition now and when I had first seen her from my hiding place in the net bin aboard the *Cicely* was astonishing, and I remembered how trim and efficient she had looked when she had fired at me as she set out after the *Bernadette*. In a few minutes the shore batteries had turned the fighting machine into a wreck seemingly uninterested in her own survival. Though the *Iroise* had been damaged and men had been killed or wounded aboard her, she was still a warship, still a recognisable entity with hope and purpose. In contrast the *Waterwitch* seemed to have crossed over some intangible boundary and had turned into something else, something that had expended all its energy and wished for nothing.

The first grim business was burial of the dead in accordance with Navy regulations. One by one, sewn up in canvas or hammocks, the victims of Morlaix were committed to the deep, each weighted with a roundshot to make him sink. Then attention was paid to the living. The *Iroise's* galley fires provided a meal for both ships' companies and a ration of rum was served. Wounded men from the *Waterwitch* were transferred to the *Iroise* and able-bodied men went in the other direction. The clanking of the *Waterwitch's* pumps, manned by the *Iroise's* people, became more urgent. I thought of my voyage in the *Jean René* and decided that pumping a frigate was easier than bailing a fishing boat single handed.

The carpenters crawled around the ship's hull with their gangs, plugging holes where they could. The ship was particularly badly holed under the waterline in the stern, and with great difficulty a sail was drawn under the hull so that the inrush of water forced it against the planking, reducing the leak considerably. Slowly the ship began to rise out of the water. The broken wheel and steering gear were repaired. At midnight, when the work was stopped, the *Waterwitch* had turned from a hulk back into a ship, a damaged ship admittedly, but a living ship with hope.

But, as the saying goes, 'It's not the ships, it's the men in 'em.' The crew had changed as well, and now moved purposefully about their tasks. The *Waterwitch's* crew had been together for a long time and there were few pressed men among them. Captain Watts, with his reputation as a man with a nose for prizes, had no trouble in attracting crews. When the work was stopped for the night the crew had again become a cohesive entity, bound by the traditions and discipline of the service and the instinct of the seaman to look after his ship.

The tow was not resumed, however. In order to rest the men the two ships spent the night lashed together, the *Iroise* under very easy sail. In retrospect, Wellstead's dictum about the fair wind should have been followed, for its neglect nearly brought about our ruin. In war, and as I have found out subsequently in business, every advantage must be exploited without delay, despite weariness. You may put things off until tomorrow, but if you do you cede the advantage to your energetic enemy or competitor.

On the following morning the ships were brought to quarters before dawn. If the mood in the midshipmen's berth was any guide, though, this was done with a feeling of resignation, of following routine. We had battled through and the ordeal was over. I had now attached myself to Snowden, who was and is as fine a shipmate as I have ever sailed with, and went with him to his station by the signal halyards.

As dawn broke, however, a sail was sighted about three or four miles south of us, and I realised with a start that it was the *Bernadette*. She had already seen us and was heading in our direction under full sail, probably delighted to see her old enemy, the *Waterwitch*, in such distress. I knew that even in our weakened condition we were more than a match for the ketch, so did not worry unduly.

'That's the *Bernadette*,' I said to Snowden. 'I hope she comes closer so we can give her something to remember!'

He looked at me in surprise. 'It's not like that, Jack. Look at her yardarm, she's signalling. She's in sight of something we can't see over the horizon.' He looked towards the horizon, just as there was a shout from the masthead, and gave me a meaningful look as the lookout called down, 'On deck there. Three sail visible dead astern. Looks like French frigates.'

We looked astern and there, hull down, were the sails of three substantial ships. The ketch was overhauling us quite quickly and was now about a mile astern, the tricouleur flying from her mizzen peak and signal flags going up and down the halyard as she signalled to the frigates. Snowden inspected the frigates through the telescope.

'They're signalling back, they know we're here.'

With great haste, for everybody knew the danger we were in, the *Waterwitch* was cast off from the *Iroise* and the tow resumed. Full sail was got on the *Iroise* and soon the ships were moving well through the water, though considerably more slowly than would have been the case if they had been sailing independently. There was a good deal of activity on the *Waterwitch*, rigging jury masts near the stumps of the old ones, for any sail that she could set would aid progress. There was a cheer from the *Iroise's* company as a temporary mast, improvised from a mainyard, was raised and a greater cheer when a large ensign was hoisted on it. The ketch was now about a mile to windward of us, on our port beam. Our port battery fired, but the range was excessive and seemed to do no damage.

'Just to keep 'em honest,' explained Snowden.

For the next hour nothing changed, the ketch overhauling us slowly and the French frigates astern gradually closing the distance. I began to be hopeful that we had escaped and that soon we would see England or perhaps friendly ships. I think by this time the *Bernadette* was about half a mile distant, keeping station ahead of our port beam, when suddenly we saw her alter course as though to cut across the *Iroise's* bows. In the few minutes as we watched her approach, we all thought that she was trying a 'crossing the T' manoeuvre, although for a ketch to attack a frigate, even from ahead, was foolish in the extreme.

The guns of both ships' broadsides were able to fire on her as she approached, until she was a few hundred yards away, when they could no longer bear. She was moving quickly, though, and weaving, and made a difficult target. Some shot must have hit her, but I do not know how much. It did not check her progress in any event. She crossed ahead of us, perhaps a hundred yards distant. We had expected her to fire as she came ahead of us, but she did not. We were further surprised when she did not continue away from us but instead gybed with a great crashing noise, men with muskets and pistols climbing quickly into the shrouds. Suddenly she was running close along our starboard side, astonishingly close, inches away, the noise of her wash filling the air. Our starboard battery was taken by surprise, as they had been readying themselves for a long shot. They fired once or twice, but the *Bernadette* was so close that the balls passed cleanly over her deck.

The men in the ketch's rigging, so close that I felt I could reach out and touch them, were firing their small arms and the balls whistled about Snowden and me. Several men on the deck fell to the sharpshooters, including the helmsmen and several officers. And then the main armament of the ketch fired. It was not much, as naval ordnance goes, but the range was point blank, they were firing directly into the crowded gun deck, and the damage that the small guns inflicted was terrible.

Then the ketch was past and I saw her round up into the wind, sails flogging. For the first time I noticed that her anchor was lowered and, as I watched, a man hanging over the bulwarks signalled aft and men at the capstan ran round, pulling up the anchor with our tow rope snagged in its flukes. As it came up, the man at the bulwark lowered himself over it, holding on to the ship with one hand and furiously chopping at the dripping rope with an axe in his other hand. In a few seconds the tow rope was cut and dropped into the sea, and the ketch backed her foresails and made off ahead of the *Waterwitch*, which carried her way and nearly caught up with the ketch.

As the *Bernadette* hauled off, the *Iroise*, with nobody at the wheel and free of the towline, rounded up into the wind. Snowden and the two ratings under his command ran to the helm, but by the time they got there the ship was up into the wind, her sails aback, and confusion on her decks. Martin, who had survived the sharpshooters unscathed, started to give orders, but as the frigate was brought under control there were shouts of 'Fire!' from down below, and we could see smoke coming from the hatches and then men emerged, coughing and eyes watering. Snowden, who was back at his post coding and hoisting shouted above the noise, 'Heated shot', and I realised that the balls the *Bernadette* had shot into the frigate had been heated in a furnace before being fired, and the red-hot shot had started fires in the crowded gun deck.

The ship was now on the starboard tack, heading back towards the wallowing *Waterwitch* but also towards France and the pursuing frigates, whose hulls were now clearly visible. As the men were organised into a chain passing buckets of seawater below to the fire, the ship was tacked and sailed close to the *Waterwitch*. The towline was passed, and within fifteen minutes the two ships were back on course towards England. The *Bernadette* had struck an audacious and effective blow, however. Though the two ships were under way, with every stitch of the *Iroise's* canvas set and the fires extinguished, the pursuing frigates were much closer. The fifteen minutes' enforced stop had gained the pursuers nearly two miles, and we could make out their details clearly and see the large tricouleurs flying from their masts. The *Bernadette* kept station with us, a mile or two distant, occasionally signalling to the French frigates. How we longed to go after her!

It became a grim race between us and our pursuers, with the French gaining on us relentlessly. The game was not without danger for the French, however, as they were far from their base in the aptly named English Channel. Our salvation was heralded by a shout from the masthead.

'On deck there. Squadron of ships two points on the starboard bow.' They could only be English. 'Looks a battleship and four frigates – the *Imperieuse*.'

Snowden must have seen the startled look on my face at the French name. 'Don't worry, she's one of ours. Don't know how she got the name.'

The conversation was cut short by a hearty cheer from the *Iroise's* company, and then Snowden and his ratings were busy signalling. *Iroise to Imperieuse three enemy frigates bearing south 5 miles.*

Snowden studied the battleship, now visible from deck level, intently through his telescope.

Acknowledge what is condition of HRH? This was a reference to the Duke.

HRH well.
Acknowledge.
Have Waterwitch in tow.
Do you require assistance?
No please pursue enemy.
Acknowledge.

That was the end of the action as far as the *Iroise* and *Waterwitch* were concerned. We saw signals hoisted on the ketch as she bore away, and in response the French frigates turned and headed for home. The English squadron passed a couple of miles to leeward, moving quickly in pursuit of the French, but we knew they had little chance of catching them. Shortly afterwards we saw the coast of England, and by nine that evening we made our way up the Needles Channel, through Hurst Narrows and into the Solent, rounding up to anchor for the night off Hurst Castle, as we had done in the poor *Cicely*, seemingly so long ago.

Despite the sombre and exhausted atmosphere of the midshipmen's berth that evening I knew that I would miss the company of Snowden and his fellows when I left the *Iroise*.

Chapter 17
Portsmouth

With a pleasant westerly breeze behind us we towed the *Waterwitch* up the Solent, passing the fleet at anchor at Spithead by mid-morning, with guns fired as salutes. By the afternoon both ships were alongside the quay at Portsmouth. Wounded men were taken ashore and the ships inspected by dockyard officers. I was looking forward to spending that evening with the midshipmen but was told that I would be required to give an account of my adventures to the Admiral and his staff that evening. A few weeks previously the prospect of reporting to an Admiral would have filled me with trepidation, but after recent events I felt no fear.

About seven o'clock I went with Midshipman Snowden to a large house near where the ship was berthed. We waited in a room adjacent to the one where the Admiral was entertaining, listening to the buzz of conversation. White-coated stewards gave us food. As usual Snowden was doing his best to overhear all that he could, and so was a quiet companion, motioning me to silence when I tried to speak. He had a well-developed talent for eavesdropping, which he has since put to good use in the King's service.

After some time I was called into the room. At a long table covered in a white cloth sat a number of naval officers including Captain Martin and the Duke. Some of them were quite elderly, portly and with grey hair. Captain Martin introduced me with some flattering words and then asked me to give an account of what I had done until I boarded the *Iroise*. At first having the eyes of all those officers on me made me unable to speak, but Captain Martin prompted me and before long I was speaking freely. There were occasional requests to 'Speak up, lad' and congratulatory interjections from time to time, and once or twice Martin reminded me of incidents I had forgotten. I was interrupted on numerous occasions by questions, but eventually my performance came to an end and, exhausted, I think I would have fallen down if I not for a firm grip on a chair.

Captain Martin stood up. 'Gentlemen, I think you'll agree that this young man has shown exceptional courage and resourcefulness, and I would like to express my thanks on behalf of *Iroise*.' He paused and looked around. 'I would also like to say that I believe that the Navy could make good use of his services. I would certainly be happy to have him in my ship.'

The Admiral replied, 'Thank you, Captain Martin, I believe you are quite right. It is not often that a young man is of such service to his country and his sovereign. I will ensure that before he leaves Portsmouth he is furnished with a letter of recommendation which he can present to Their Lordships should he wish to take up a midshipman's berth in future, and I will further recommend that he is credited with a year's service.'

I don't know if there was an element of competition in the proceedings, each wishing to appear as generous as the other, or whether they really were grateful to me, feelings probably partly engendered by plentiful food and drink, but to my astonishment the Duke got to his feet.

'I would also like to express my thanks. Your actions undoubtedly saved the King from real danger and did considerable damage to his enemies, and I am sure that in return the King would wish to make some appropriate gesture.'

I was then shown out of the room, and walked back to the ship in a blur of unreality, blurting out what had happened to Snowden in such a jumbled torrent of words that he made me repeat it several times before he fully understood their meaning. His expressions of amazement and astonishment at my luck were repeated by the other midshipmen when I got back into the berth, and there was much ribbing at my expense and frequent mocking references to 'Lord Stone of Portland' or 'Lord Portland Stone'. Those few hours in the midshipmen's berth alongside at Portsmouth were amongst the most enjoyable I had spent in my life, and when I got into my hammock I was sure that I wanted to join the Navy and become a midshipman in the *Iroise*, and I felt truly contented that I was to be given the opportunity.

At about twelve o'clock the next day I was called to see the Captain in his cabin. The sailors and the dockyard hands had been busy, and the cabin bore no resemblance to the place it had been during the battle, except for the distinct smell of smoke.

'Jack,' said the Captain, indicating that I should sit at the table and taking out a letter. 'I have here the letter from Admiral Hood and need hardly say that Their Lordships are unlikely to ignore such a recommendation from the Admiral. If you do wish to avail yourself of this opportunity, I would be happy to give you a berth in this ship. Do not make your mind up straight away but decide once you have spent some time at home. The ship will be in Portsmouth for at least two months.'

I think Wellstead would have classed this as a fair wind, and I had no intention of wasting it. To become a midshipman in the *Iroise* was all that I wanted. I had no particular desire to experience more fighting, but reasoned that fighting was not in my mind when I had signed Wellstead's articles, and if I fought as a member of the *Iroise's* company at least it would not be alone, as on a merchant ship.

I spoke up as loud and confidently as I could. 'Sir, I am very grateful to you and the Navy and can think of nothing I would rather do. I do not need any additional time to consider. I am apprenticed to Mr Wellstead, but as he is in a French prison and his ship is destroyed I do not consider that this is still an obligation upon me.'

Captain Martin got to his feet. 'Well said, Jack. I won't shake your hand, for obvious reasons.' At this he looked at his injured arm and my broken fingers. 'I'll expect you to join the ship before we leave Portsmouth then.'

He walked with me to the door, then added, 'I've asked Mr Badcock to take you to Weymouth in the pinnace tomorrow if this wind holds.'

I passed another congenial evening in the midshipmen's berth, thinking constantly that this would soon be my home and these fellows with whom I had shared so much danger would be my companions. It seemed too good to be true.

We set off early the next morning, in a brisk southerly wind. The pinnace was commanded by Midshipman Badcock and there were six sailors. We rowed out of Portsmouth harbour, crowded with ships, hoisted the sails at the entrance and headed westward through the Solent. Before long we had the tide under us and by ten in the morning we were off Lymington, when I suddenly remembered Nat, the seaman from the *Cicely* who we had left in Milford. I told Badcock that I had promised Nat that the *Cicely* would stop for him, and that as the *Cicely* no longer existed and I was the only member of the crew in England, I would like to go and offer him passage home if he was still there.

Badcock, always one for an adventure, no matter how small, took the pinnace into the river, which I had never seen in daytime, and we sailed and rowed up to the small village of Keyhaven. In the company of Badcock and four sailors, I walked up the narrow road away from the shore, passing the spot where we had had the confrontation with the Revenue that night. I cannot say that the inhabitants of Keyhaven or Milford welcomed us with open arms, in fact the streets and roads were deserted. In those days, groups of Royal Navy sailors ashore often meant the press gang, something much to be feared by merchant seamen and fishermen.

Our group went up to the Doctor's house, and he appeared at the door. He did not recognise me, but remembered our arrival that night very well indeed, and took us across the green to the house where Nat was being nursed. Nat had mended well, though he still could not walk and had no recollection of his fall on the *Cicely* or his arrival in Milford. A cart was borrowed from a local inhabitant, who refused any payment, I think on the grounds that the possible loss of a cart was a price well worth paying if it got us out of the village.

With Nat a passenger, we sailed in the pinnace out through Hurst Narrows and set a course for Portland. In the brisk southerly wind and sunshine the passage was fast and easy and I watched with great satisfaction as the Dorset coast slid by. I must admit I felt a slight pang of regret that we would not be stopping at Kimmeridge as we passed it in the last of the light, but this was soon forgotten as we approached Portland.

At about midnight the boat grounded on Castletown beach. I said my farewells to Badcock, Nat and the men and set out to walk home.

Epilogue

And that is all there is to relate. For a month I stayed with my parents on Portland while I recovered my strength and my hand and head mended. My dreams gradually became less vivid. I visited Wellstead's wife, cold and stony faced in her house, to tell her what I knew of her husband.

One pleasant day my father and I sailed our boat across to Kimmeridge Bay, where I remade the acquaintance of Lizzie, who seemed pleased to see me. We walked along the beach in the company of her father and inspected the wreckage of the *Jean René*, lying broken on the rocks of Brandy Bay. It seemed a shame that the boat that had served me so well would so quickly end up as firewood, but she was completely past saving.

Lizzie looked disconsolate as she stood on the beach waving goodbye, and I felt the same as I looked back and vowed that I would return to see her before I joined my ship. That I did make the return trip is a matter of record.

After a month I made my way back to Portsmouth, and joined the *Iroise*, splendidly repaired, as Midshipman Stone. My naval career had begun.

***

Wellstead and the *Cicely's* crew did not have to wait long in their French prison, for they were freed as a result of the peace of 1802.

About the Author

Born in Swanage, Paul Weston went to sea as an engineer apprentice with the BP Tanker Company. His subsequent seafaring career included spells with European Ferries and P&O. After leaving the sea and graduating from university with a degree in mechanical engineering he worked for the Bermuda Electric Light Company and Lloyd's Register of Shipping.

Paul started and ran Weston Antennas for 20 years, designing and manufacturing large satellite earth station antennas in Piddlehinton, Dorset, and installing them around the world. He left the firm following a dispute with its venture capitalist investors, and now works sedately as a design engineer with Siemens.

Paul has extensive sailing experience, including a trip from New York to Lymington in a home-designed and built 26-ft boat, and currently owns a Mitchell Sea Angler which he keeps at Wareham.

He lives in rural Dorset with his wife and two children, and is currently working on two writing projects, one of which develops Jack Stone's later career, and another more contemporary story.

Glossary

Assize – trial conducted by circuit judges.

barque – sailing ship with three masts, the forward two with square sails, and the aftermast rigged fore and aft.

Battle of the Saints (Saintes) – naval battle fought between the British under Admiral Rodney and the French under the Comte de Grasse. The Saintes are islands near Dominica in the Caribbean.

blockade – during the French Revolutionary Wars the Royal Navy closely blockaded the entire French coast for many years, winter and summer – an outstanding display of seamanship and determination which had the side effect of making the Navy extremely efficient, in contrast to its French counterpart which was bottled up in port.

Board of Trade – department of the British Government which became responsible for enforcing the Merchant Shipping Act later in the nineteenth century.

bosun (boatswain) – senior seaman.

braces – ropes to control the yards which support a ship's square sails; hence 'lee braces' are braces on the side of the ship away from the wind.

broach – when a vessel is running before the wind, following waves may push the stern of the vessel to the side. This can be very dangerous and may lead to a capsize or swamping.

capstan – winch with vertical axis. The *Cicely*'s capstan was driven by men pushing wooden bars as they walked around it.

carron (carronade) – a gun manufactured by the Carron Ironworks of Scotland. The company was founded in 1789 and now manufactures domestic sinks.

Carteret – port on the western side of the Cotentin Peninsular noted for its exceptional tides and vast sandy beaches.

chasse-marée – literally 'tide chaser', a heavily canvassed French vessel used for smuggling and similar activities.

Chesil Beach – a long shingle spit which joins Portland to the mainland. With the wind from the west or south-west it forms a lee shore, especially for vessels proceeding up the English Channel. The beach is very steep, and the undertow from the surf in rough conditions makes escaping from the sea very difficult.

coaming – vertical edge of a hatch or cockpit.

coasting – trading along the coast rather than 'deep sea'. In British ships coasting is traditionally limited to the area between Brest and the Elbe.

cockpit sole – the 'floor' of the cockpit.

coney – rabbit.

davit – small gooseneck crane from which ships' boats are suspended by rope 'falls'. Davits are usually arranged in pairs and are able to swivel so that the boat can be moved from the ship's deck to its side – hence 'swing out the boats'.

fluke – the part of an anchor that digs into the ground.

fo'c'stle – (abbreviation of 'forecastle') accommodation at the fore part of the ship where the crew lived 'before the mast', as opposed to the officers living in the aft end of the ship.

frigate – fast, lightly armed warship.

grapnel – large hook with two or more tines.

Hard Times of Old England – English folk song. An interesting modern version is sung by Imagined Village.

Heart of Oak – official march of the Royal Navy, composed by William Boyce in 1759 with lyrics by David Garrick.

heaving line – thin rope used for throwing from one vessel to another.

helm down – turning the ship's head into the wind.

helm up – turning the ship's head away from the wind.

in irons – ship stationary and pointing directly into the wind with the sails flapping.

Iroise – Royal Navy frigate which had been captured from the French. French ships captured by the Royal Navy generally continued to use their original names.

ketch – definition varies with time, but in the novel refers to small sailing vessel with two fore and aft rigged masts, the aftermost of which is the smallest.

King – in *Weymouth Bound* the king referred to is George III, 'Farmer George'. George was very fond of Weymouth and spent long periods there. As described in the book, he was renowned as an early riser.

landing – smuggling contraband ashore.

Leave Her Johnny – chanty with improvised derogatory words about the ship and officers traditionally sung when the crew is about to pay off at the end of a voyage. Perhaps the most authentic version was recorded by Bob Roberts.

leeboard – board at the side of a vessel which is lowered to reduce leeway, the tendency of the sails to drive the vessel sideways rather than forward. Similar in principle to the centreboard of a sailing dinghy.

Lilli Bulero – satirical ballad about Ireland. Signature tune of the BBC World Service.

lugger – a vessel, generally a small one, propelled by a lugsail, rather than a gaff mainsail.

main topsail – upper sail on the main mast of the *Cicely*.

midshipman – trainee officer in the Royal Navy.

mizzen – aftermost mast of a ship.

mole – protective stone jetty around a harbour.

pawl – ratchet.

pinnace – boat carried by a ship, principally driven by oars.

Pool of London – part of the River Thames below London Bridge where ships worked their cargo.

Popham – Royal Navy signal code devised by Admiral Sir Home Riggs Popham KCB, a naval officer who led a varied and interesting life.

port (starboard) tack – ship sailing so that the wind is coming from the port (starboard) side.

prize money – when an enemy ship was captured the value of the ship was assessed by a prize court and the proceeds shared between the officers and crew of the capturing ship.

race (tide race) – an area of confused breaking seas caused by the tidal stream running strongly over obstructions. Two races feature in the book: the Portland Race, an area off the tip of the Isle of Portland, and the Race of Alderney, between Alderney and the adjacent coast of France. Both are extremely dangerous in some states of wind and tide. In the Race of Alderney, off La Foraine beacon, the tide can run at up to nine knots.

reefed mizzen – the mizzen sail is the aftermost fore and aft sail on the ship. When the wind is strong sails are reduced in size (reefed).

Revenue cutter – small ship used to supress smuggling.

scandalised mainsail – reducing the power of the mainsail by lowering the peak of the gaff.

schooner – vessel with two or more masts, predominantly fore and aft rigged. The foremast is smaller than the mainmast.

scuppers – drains.

sheerline – the line of the deck when the ship is viewed in side profile.

spritsail – a sail with a diagonal wooden spar known as a 'sprit', commonly used as the mainsail on Thames barges.

steep to – coast with deep water close to the shore.

swivel – gun supported on a mount which allows it to be aimed easily.

tack – turn the ship through the wind.

tailed on the grass line – a 'grass' line is a rope made from coir or coconut fibre. Coir fibre is light and ropes made from it float, making it very useful in some circumstances. To 'tail' means to pull a rope manually, rather than use a winch.

tiller – lever attached to the rudder which is used to steer the craft.

wherry – vessel used for river transport.

William – third son of George III. He spent a considerable time in the Royal Navy and was a friend of Nelson. The Duke of Clarence, he later became William IV and was nicknamed 'the Sailor King'.